FREEDOM FROM FEARS

"A Foolproof Guide to Overcoming Your Fears"

ALAIN LEA

Published by Christ In All Nations
A division of Christ In All Nations Group
P.O Box 588, Granger, Indiana 46530, USA.
www.christinallnations.org

Printed in the United States of America

ISBN: 978-1-952806-17-9 (paperback)
ISBN: 978-1-952806-18-6 (Kindle)
ISBN: 978-1-952806-12-4 (hardback)
ISBN: 978-1-952806-13-1 (audio)

Table of Contents

SECTION 1   7

Introduction   8

Understanding Fear   9

The Origins of Fear   12

The Mechanics of Fear   15

The Importance of Overcoming Fear   20

Types of fear   25

A Close-up Look at Fear   29

Fear of Death   31

Fear of the Unknown   37

Fear of Failure   39

Fear of Rejection   47

Fear of Insufficiency   51

Fear of Man   58

SECTION 2   67

Introduction   68

We are not meant to live in fear   69

The Fear of God   74

Overcoming Our Fear of God   78

SECTION 3   83

Introduction   84

The Consequences of Fear   85

Fear Forces Us to Live Out of a Mistaken Identity   90

Made for love   93

Taking the Leap from Fear to Love   96

True faith   98

Final Words   101

Acknowledgement   102

About the Author   106

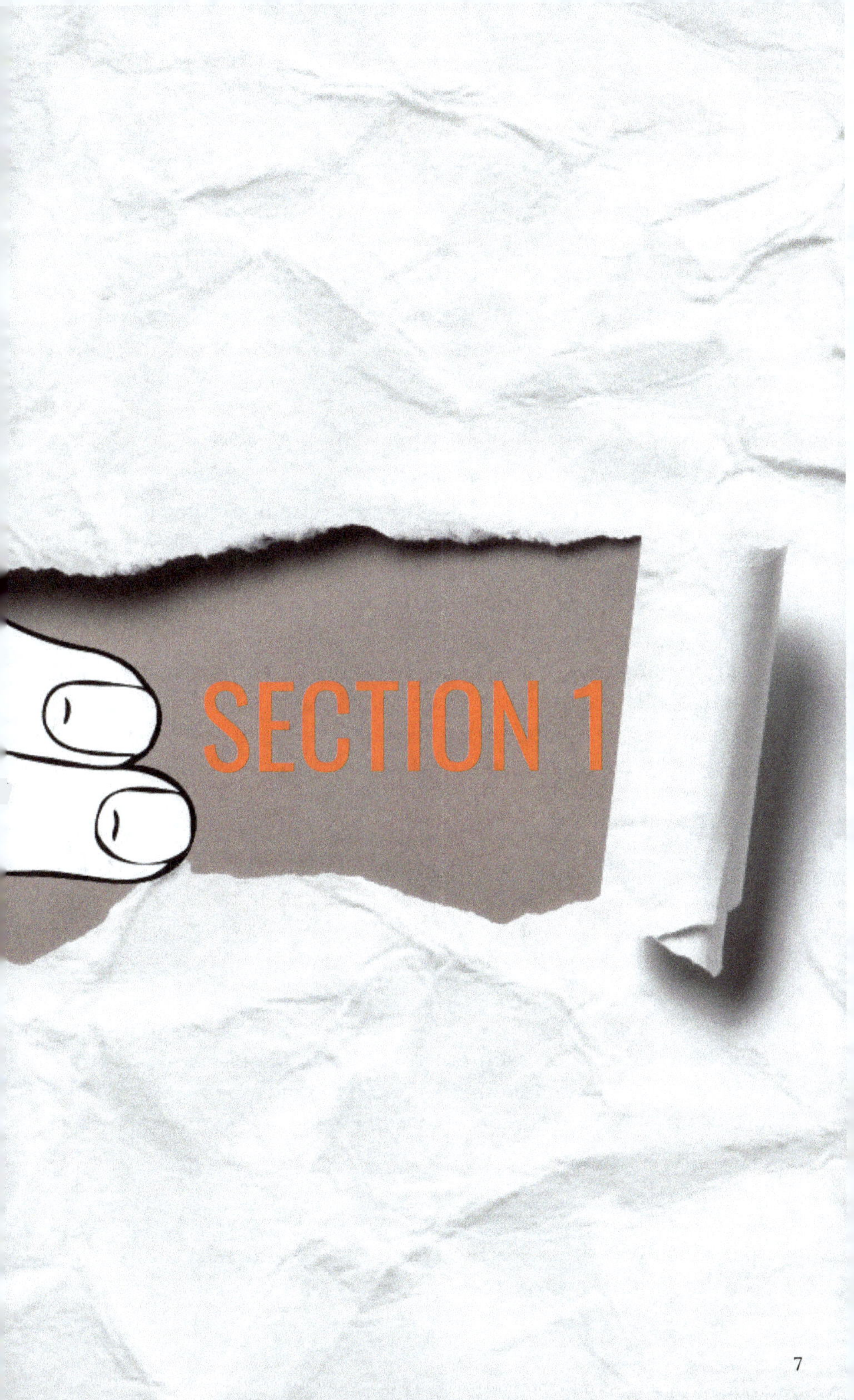
SECTION 1

Introduction

Imagine a world without color. Boring, monotonous, dull...are some of the words that spring up to mind. Simplistically speaking, just as colors make up this world, emotions color every moment of human existence. Happiness, pain, fear, anger, hate, peace, calm...most of our living moments are tinged with one or the other of these emotions or feelings. More often than not, a combination of these feelings too.

Now, emotions are basically feelings generated within us and define our persona which in turn molds our equations with others. By extension, our emotions decide the greater direction of our lives. Emotions can be broadly classified as positive and negative vibrations; good and bad feelings. Good vibes lead to good consequences while the bad ones take us towards unhappy consequences.

Of all the emotions, it is the one we know as 'FEAR' that causes the most trouble and damage. From fear springs anger, and thereon it transforms into hate. From here on, it's but one simple step to harboring evil thoughts, and the descent to moral degeneration.

In my years with helping people from different walks of life, I have regularly come across fear as the common factor behind the problems such people faced. Fear is like the valve that uncorks the flood of problems. Handle it wisely and intelligently and see your problems reduce and die away. It can be as simple as that.

Looking at how common a factor, this dreadful feeling that fear is, I felt it necessary to reach out to all those people who face these problems, want to handle them but don't know how to. My book is a sincere attempt to reach out to all such people whom I cannot meet physically.

Over the next few pages, we'll take a look at the various facets and dimensions of fear, the ways and means to address our fears in a realistic world to emerge fearless and happy.

Understanding Fear

The year was 1988. The setting was the diving preliminary rounds of the Seoul Olympics. All eyes were on a young American Greg Louganis as he made his way up the diving board and executed a 2 ½ reverse pike maneuver. And then the unthinkable happened. He dove off the springboard, rose in the air and as he came down pirouetting, his had banged into the wooden board with a sickening thud! Greg dropped into the waters far below, surfaced and swam back to the ground. The collective gasp of surprise and shock dissolved into uncertainty over Greg's continuance in the sporting event.

But to everyone's chagrin, Greg was soon back on the diving board and went on to win to gold medals in the 1988 Olympics diving events.

Sports commentators, sports lovers and diving aficionados watched the video repeatedly, attempting to analyze and understand what went wrong. On his part, Greg later told the press that he didn't watch the video. He simple shoved the mishap and its memories to the back of his mind and went back to the diving board with a clean slate. The rest as they say is History, with a capital h.

To me personally, Greg's comeback is an outstanding example of human beings overcoming their fears and going on to win fame and fortune.

Well, all of us are not Greg Louganis, but yes, we all face fears in our daily lives, in some form or the other. While some fears are inconsequential, some keep on niggling at us over the years, while there are certain cases which are overwhelming in nature with possibly life-changing consequences. On the same note, all of us have different ways of tackling this quintessential problem dubbed 'FEAR'. Some ignore it, some agonize over it, some handle it, some look for help while many succumb to it.

Before looking for solutions, we need to understand causes. So, let's begin with trying to understand what fear is....

Scientifically speaking, fear is a biochemical response that is present in most living beings. Apart from this universal response mechanism, in humans, fear is also an emotional response that differs from person to person. The fear response in humans is dependent upon a variety of factors and situations that we find ourselves in during the course of our lives.

Common indicators of fear range from a shortness of breath and dry mouth to speeding heartbeat, nausea and upset stomach. In severe cases, fear can lead to strokes and heart attacks too. Fear can result in panic attacks, social anxiety disorders and a host of other phobias too.

The emotion of fear is responsible for the 'fight or flee' reaction that is seen in animals. However, it's a slightly different story when it comes to us, human beings. Instead of fight or flee, most of us tend to fester in fear, ultimately resulting in the cascading of unpleasant consequences – physical health, mental well-being, emotional balance, financial difficulties, failing relationships, professional failures...the list can go on and on.

The funny thing is, fear - a small word that enjoys a big reputation. People consider fear as a sign of weakness, as something to avoid at all costs. No one wants to live in fear. If you asked a person on the street if they'd rather be afraid or fearless, the large majority of people would tell you they want to be fearless. The good news is, we can confront our fears and emerge victorious. But more of that later...

Another thing to remember is that fear can be triggered by real threats as well as imagined or contrived ones. Usually, fear is not a pleasant sensation. Of course, some experiences could provide a small adrenaline rush that exhilarates us. For example, visits to scary movies or haunted houses are associated with a pleasant experience of fear. But most of the situations where people enjoy feeling afraid, are controlled and anticipated experiences, often containing little or no prospects of real fear. Imagine differently you'd feel in a haunted house if it caught fire and you were trapped inside. Remember, feeling shocked or surprised for entertainment purposes is far different from that of the pains experienced in real life. The fact is, people do not relish the feeling of real fear that arises when facing danger or pain.

So, to begin with, there's fear and then there's real fear. To address your fears, you need to distinguish between the two types.

Fear also comes in different sizes and shapes. The disagreeable sensation that fear brings upon us, has several ranges of severity. It may be a temporary feeling like thinking you're going to be in a car accident, then avoiding it. That fear may only last seconds. You might experience a low level of fear in your everyday life that's more constant. This is often referred to as stress or anxiety. Both stress and anxiety are types of fear, but come from more of a perceived fear than that of actual danger. The danger with the feeling of stress is that it's such a low level of fear that we end up ignoring or accepting it as normal. But this can lead to health issues, even if the fear isn't very strong, because it is a constant and ongoing feeling that our bodies are not meant to sustain in the long run.

Fear could also become so intense as to cause physical issues like panic attacks or an elevated heart rate. Fear can turn out to be deadly if strong enough. Fear can even cause permanent damage to a person. If someone experiences something horrific, such as a physical attack or prolonged abuse, fear can actually rewire the brain and cause a variety of issues that may require professional help to overcome. Even the more subtle types of fear in the form of stress or anxiety can cause damage to a person over time, leading to problems with physical and mental health. (995 words)

KEY TAKEAWAYS

1. The emotion of fear is responsible for the 'fight or flee' reaction that is seen in animals.
2. The good news is that we can confront our fears and emerge victorious.
3. Fear also comes in different sizes and shapes.

The Origins of Fear

Remember the first time you experienced fear in your life? The likely answer would probably take you back to those distant memories of your childhood when you first began going to school. For most people, it is usually those first days in school that stand out as the first memories of feeling fear. No wonder, being plucked from the secure confines of your home and the comforting presence of family, you suddenly find yourself in the midst of strangers.

Interestingly, we are unaware of it but our tryst with fear begins the moment we are born. Researchers have identified two fears that humans are born with – of falling, and loud sounds.

According to scientists, the fear of falling is a basic survival instinct for many species. Similarly, the fear of loud sounds, scientifically termed as acoustic startle reflex, assists in honing 'the fight or flight' responses in humans and most living beings.

Going back to our childhood memories of school, it was certainly, a traumatic experience for most! But as time passes by, you soon adjust to the new normal and begin enjoying the experiences. Over time, you outgrow these initial fears but encounter new situations that fill you with dread. Some fears vanish with time, while some remain to haunt you for longer periods or even your entire life.

As you can see, fear and human existence are intertwined. The trick is to know what fears to let go and which ones to tackle and emerge a better human being.

Most people would agree that they want to be free of fear in their lives, but being fearless isn't the same thing as living life with no fear. You'll never be able to remove all fear from your life. Being fearless is what happens when you know how to use fear to your benefit. It may seem impossible, but you can accomplish this once you understand a few things about fear.

Fear is often thought of as an automatic response. You hear a strange noise; you instantly feel a jolt of fear. A questionable looking person walks down the street toward you, and fear shows up again. But fear is not automatic. There is an instinctual fear born into all humans, although most fears are taught or learned.

Instinctual fear is necessary for survival. This type of fear keeps a person from being too reckless and helps to avoid fates like being mauled by tigers. It's a self-preservation feature that is built into the basic wiring of our brains. It's also what makes a person respond to a fearful thing by fighting back, fleeing away, or freezing up. This type of fear is important because it helps to keep you safe and alive.

Acquired fear comes from years of being told that you should be afraid of something. As children, it was parents or teachers teaching things like running with scissors could be harmful. They may have probably taught us that strangers should be feared as they can cause harm. Some of these fears are important. Children need to be taught that running into traffic could get them hurt, and it's better for them to be taught this rather than to learn it through experience. However, there are many taught fears that may not be so beneficial.

Some acquired fears may also have been passed down through families, allowing unhealthy patterns to continue for generations. For example, a parent may fear going to the dentist and pass that fear onto his or her children, creating a cycle of poor dental care that benefits no one. Taught fear can also come on a larger level from society. Certain people groups may be presented as dangerous and so should be feared. This is where racism and prejudice come from. Many of these fears are unfounded or irrational, but become part of a person's psyche because they're viewed as "normal" fears within society, family, or friends.

On the other hand, learned fear comes with age and from personal experience. A child may explore new things like plugging utensils into electrical outlets. After experiencing one unpleasant electric shock, it understands that perhaps outlets are best for plugs only. But learned fear isn't limited to things that might keep a person safe. You can also learn things like distrust. Maybe a friend betrayed you or told a secret and that led you to fear opening up to people. Learned fear can be beneficial, but needn't be so always.

Learned fear may be the hardest to overcome because it usually sets in as a result of personal experience. Once someone has experienced something painful, whether physically or emotionally, it's difficult to overcome because he or she remembers that fear and will retain the desire and instinct to avoid the pain felt from the experience. Learned fears are also often the most damaging. They can form in irrational ways, can keep you from being close to people, from trying new experiences, or from stepping out in faith to do something you find intimidating. (585 words)

KEY TAKEAWAYS

1. Our tryst with fear begins the moment we are born.

2. Instinctual fear is necessary for survival.

3. Learned fears are often the most damaging ones.

The Mechanics of Fear

Fear isn't a stand-alone emotion. It builds upon itself and on other feelings. The more afraid you are, the more fear you'll feel. Any additional fear response will amplify what you're already feeling, increasing your overall fear. Being in a heightened state of awareness can make even harmless things feel scary. For example, if you watched a documentary on venomous spiders and have a fear of spiders, the shirt tag tickling your neck may suddenly feel like a crawling spider, causing you to react with fear to something absolutely harmless. A knock on the door while watching a horror movie may be enough to make a person scream in terror when they would normally have no response other than to walk toward the door while quietly wondering who could be on the other side.

If you're forced into an experience that triggers a learned or taught fear, this can be an even more dramatic experience. For a person with a fear of flying, any little bump of turbulence during a plane ride can cause extreme anxiety. The brain is activating all the previous fear responses to the experience of flying and using imagination to create a scenario that feels like the end of the world is near. For someone without this fear, they may not even notice the small bump that caused the person sitting beside them to break out into a sweat and tighten their seatbelt. Likewise, a person fearful of losing his job may experience intense anxiety at being called into the boss's office, even if it's for nothing more than a mundane meeting. Brains that are already fearful will have a stronger response to anything that seems to feed that particular fear.

Fear is a strong emotion that causes a variety of reactions. The four common types of reactions to fear are freeze, fight or flight and fright. You've likely experienced one or many of these when faced with fear.

'Fright' is the common "deer in the headlights" response. The situation seems so overwhelming that your mind panics so much that you can't decide what to do next. Instead of acting, you become consumed by the fear and end up doing nothing. For example, if you received a memo that the company you work for is planning several layoffs in the upcoming week, fright would cause you to lose sleep and appetite, have an elevated heart rate and limited brain function, yet do nothing to improve the situation. This reaction would make you unable to think clearly and respond effectively. Feeling fright, for long enough, leads to hopelessness and depression.

The fright response would end up leaving a person to do nothing more than worry, sitting and waiting to get a phone call to come to the boss's office. It is an unproductive response and leads to a hindered emotional state. In fact, this response may actually make the situation worse. Perhaps the company is deciding between two candidates. One has acted like the model employee in the last week, while the other is a complete mess, unable to perform the job well. In this scenario, fright may become a self-fulfilling prophecy—the fear response leads to the scariest result.

The flight response is the one that leads a person to escape or get away at all costs. The impending danger is too much, so they run away from it rather than face it. Fleeing seems like the best way to avoid the pain coming from whatever caused the fear. In the example of the company layoffs, a flight response might cause the person who received the layoff email to suddenly quit. They might think there's no reason to wait around to be laid off and that their time would be better spent looking for another job.

This can be a harmful response for many reasons. It could cause a person to quit a job they never would have lost in the first place. By avoiding the perceived danger, they never stick around long enough to find out if the danger is real. It could cause a pattern of avoidance—why deal with a panful situation when you can just take off and not face it? This response can be harmful in two primary ways. One is that the person fleeing may never learn to face fear or deal with a painful situation. By always avoiding a painful situation, there is never an opportunity to work through the fear and pain. The second way it could be harmful is that running away may bring about the undesired situation faster. Quitting before you can be laid off has the same result of being without a job and eliminates any benefit that might have come from being laid off, such as severance pay or help in finding a new job.

Fighting is often not the best response, either. In the case of a physical attack, fighting back may be the best option, but this is not often true. A person who responds with fighting to a layoff email may contact the boss to complain. He might get angry and throw papers off his desk or cause an uncomfortable scene. But if he can remain calm, fighting back may instead mean having a talk with the boss and successfully convincing him to layoff someone else.

It's easy to see why fighting back can be a harmful response. Aside from the rare times when fighting back helps, this response often causes more grief in the end. Imagine a person who is afraid of flying. In the case of air turbulence, a fight response may cause the person to shove aside someone blocking the aisle out of fear they may be trapped on a plane that's going down. The scared person might cause enough commotion to be removed from the plane in order to keep others safe. A fight response could cause a parent to lash out and hit a child for doing something careless that may have gotten them hurt. Or it could lead a spouse to act abusively, which would significantly damage the marriage and both people in it, causing whatever the initial fear was to seem inconsequential to the new problem of a physical fight.

'Freezing' may be the best response to fear. This is different than reacting in fright because unlike causing a person to not react due to fear, freezing could give person enough of a pause to be able to think and act more clearly. In the layoff example discussed previously, if you reacted by freezing, you might read the email and stop whatever project you were in the middle of. It might cause you to lose focus and think of nothing but the fear you're now feeling. But it could have the positive response of allowing you to take a breather and decide how to move forward. Perhaps it's time to clean up the old resume, or maybe a heartfelt talk with management would remind them of all the ways you've been a productive employee over the years.

This isn't always beneficial, however. Some decisions need to be made quickly. If a person is faced with an out-of-control car coming for them, stopping to think about what's happening would lead him or her to be in an accident. If used wisely, the freeze response could give a person enough time to make the best decision. But it could also cause them to not make a decision at all and fail because they were too focused on the problem and didn't find a solution fast enough.

Each type of response has a time when it may be beneficial, but most of the time, these responses lead to more harm. The more focus and obsession there are over a fear, the scarier it will seem, and the more likely to cause lasting damage.

The type of threat a person faces may decide the type of response that emerges/evolves. An imagined fear often causes inaction, whereas an immediate threat results in action. A situation you worry about, that you picture happening and stress over, requires little action since the threat is only imagined. It often takes a more real threat to bring an active response. It's easy to sit around worrying all day, doing nothing about it, but if danger is knocking on your door, you'll have to do something—either address it or run and hide. An imagined fear often causes a sort of stressed-out paralysis, but on the other hand, a real threat may cause a panicked frenzy of action.

This is why reading about heart disease may not change the way a person eats, but having a heart attack will send them to the health food store and make them toss out all the fried food they've been storing in the freezer. In order to get real action, there must be a real threat. You may have heard stories of parents doing heroic actions like lifting cars to save their children. This is an impossible task that only a fear-fueled adrenaline rush could make happen. If that same parent sat and only thought about a vehicle crushing their baby, they would feel fear, but it wouldn't be enough to allow them to lift a car.

In case you're wondering as to what exactly is happening in the body when you face a potential 'fear' situation, let me explain: The process of fear begins in the brain and makes its way throughout the body to prepare it for the best fight, or flight response. The fear response takes birth in the amygdala, a region of the brain. Shaped like almonds, and located in the brain's temporal lobe, this set of nuclei specializes in estimating the emotional relevance of any stimuli we come across.

For instance, the amygdala gets into action mode whenever we see emotions on another human face. This reaction in the amygdala is more pronounced when seeing emotions like anger and fear on the other person's face. The process also involves the release of stress hormones and activation of the sympathetic nervous system.

All this activity results in bodily changes that better equip us to face danger situations. The brain turns to hyperalert mode with dilation of the pupils and the bronchi while breathing rate accelerates. The heart rate speeds up and blood pressure rises increasing blood flow and glucose supply to the skeletal muscles. Simultaneously, non-vital organs can be seen to significantly slowdown in such situations.
The amygdala works intimately with the hippocampus which is also a part of the brain. The brain uses the hippocampus and prefrontal cortex, to interpret the potential threat. Together, the two organs handle higher-level processing of context, to identify is a threat is real or perceived.

KEY TAKEAWAYS

1. Fear isn't a stand-alone emotion.

2. The four common types of reactions to fear are freeze, fight or flight and fright.

3. Feeling fright, for long enough, leads to hopelessness and depression.

The Importance of Overcoming Fear

Try to find out about their favorite childhood story, and the majority of people are sure to respond with an emphatic 'David and Goliath'. And why not? For children down the ages, the mind's eye picture of young lad David felling the mighty Goliath with a mere pebble, is a fascinating story of defiance of the odds on the path to victory.

Imagine...twice a day, Goliath would strut around, challenging the Israelites to a 1 on 1 battle. And for the Israelites it was a daily nightmare as they shrunk back in fear, mesmerized by the sheer size and power that Goliath represented, and the prospect of a painful death. None of them would dare to challenge Goliath. This went on for 40 days until young David stepped in when he heard of the reward for defeating Goliath.

While Goliath was covered in armor and held a deadly javelin, David was armed with nothing more than a staff, a sling and 5 stones. On top of that, David was but a child in size compared to the gigantic Goliath. But all these differences did not scare David away from the fight. He simply aimed for Goliath's forehead and let loose a pebble from his sling, and the rest as they say is the stuff that dreams are made of!

More than two thousand years later, David is still remembered for his heroism and is used as a case study in business administration courses too.

So, what set David apart from his compatriots? The answer is FEAR or the lack of it. While the remaining Israelis allowed their fear of defeat, dismemberment and death to hold them back, David shrugged off his fears and walked the path of faith to victory and everlasting glory.

The moral of the story is that no matter who you are, what you do, where you are from, you can overcome your fears and live a happy life.

All you need to do is take that first step towards the cure.
So, let's see how to go about conquering our fears...

At this stage, I would like to stress upon the importance of a two-pronged strategy to effectively tackle your fears and emerge victorious. Essentially, our approach involves using practical steps and complementing them with generous amounts of spiritual inputs. Believe me, there's no better support system than God and his comforting word, to drive away the demons of fear in our minds.

Step up to your fears: To step out of the shadows of fear, the first thing you need to do is to look them in the face. Avoid situations that scare you will only delay the recovery process. As a result, you only stop doing the things you must do or have to do. Moreover, you will not know for sure if your fears are real or imaginary. Remember, anxiety-related issues only tend to grow in magnitude if left unattended. That's why it makes sense to face up to your fears.

Understand yourself: Make an honest attempt to learn as much as possible about your specific fear or anxiety. Maintain an anxiety diary to record your feelings and reactions whenever, wherever you experience such situations. You can always start small by setting yourself achievable goals for tackling your apprehensions. Try carrying a list of things that help you during those instances when you tend to get frightened or anxious. Many people have found this a practical way of resolving the primary belief systems that trigger your fears and panic attacks.

Physical exercise: Regular and moderate physical exercise can be just what the doctor ordered for your fear issues. Apart from toning your body, physical workouts have a salutary effect on the mind – thanks to the beneficial hormones released by the body. Also, to do physical exercise the right way, requires a certain amount of focus and concentration, which in turn can divert your mind from negative thoughts and feelings.

Just relax: Practicing relaxation techniques is a good way to positively deal with the mental and physical characteristics of fear. Simple movements such as letting your shoulders to drop and deep breathing can help your body relax really fast. You could also explore options such as tai chi, yoga, meditation, or go in for body massage sessions.

Eat healthy: Eat plenty of fruit and vegetables while avoiding excess sugar after duly consulting your physician. Stay away from tea and coffee as much as possible since caffeine can raise anxiety levels.

No or low alcohol is a good idea: Many people find courage in a bottle of alcohol, when facing their fears or anxieties. While imbibing from this 'Dutch courage' can be a pleasurable experience, once the effects of drink wear away, you'll find the problems remain where they were. In fact, the after-effects of alcohol usage can leave you even more tensed and worried.

Faith matters: Look beyond the practical, to the spiritual, if you want to see results that are fast and enduring. One of the best and most obvious antidote to fear is to meditate on the word of God. As you meditate and realize how wonderful God actually is, you begin to gain control over your emotions, which in turn can reduce feelings of fear and anxiety. Knowing the fact that God is our protector, can relieve a lot of anxiety. We know that Jesus said His yoke is easy and His burden light (Matthew 11:30). He says cast all our cares on Him. Psalm 91 is a great chapter to meditate on.

Faith in the Almighty God provides you with the mental strength and resilience to cope with the stress and strain of everyday life. It's definitely a great idea to regularly attend church and similar faith groups.

Living your life surrounded by fears can be dangerous for you, and your loved ones. Beginning with the physical and emotional health risks involved, to the tendency of acting without enough thought, fear can end up making us do things we should usually never do. Apart from a lifetime of health issues, fear can even shorten a life span. It can make a bad situation worse or convert a perceived situation into reality. The truth is that while fear can protect you at times, it can also trap you in a cage of insecurities.

Therefore, the question is, if fear is so debilitating, how can you handle it in a way that it brings along benefits, and makes your life productive? How can you overcome the overwhelming responses that might potentially worse the situation?

The feeling we experience when something isn't correct in whatever circumstances we may find ourselves in, is God's way of trying to make us aware of what it is about or can happen if we remain where we are at that specific moment. I wouldn't call it fear. Because Jesus said I give you my peace John 14:27 and 2 Tim 1:7 Paul tells Timothy that we didn't receive the spirit of fear.

Now, here's the good news. Jesus is the answer to all our fears. Meditating on the word of Christ will keep you in perfect peace because your mind will be sound in Him and that alone guard you away from fear. God does not want you to remain trapped in fear, unable to act. Some dictionaries define fear as: "a distressing emotion aroused by impending danger, evil, pain, etc., whether the threat is real or imagined; the feeling or condition of being afraid." The Urban Dictionary defines fear further: "Fear is the mind-killer. Fear is the little death that brings total obliteration." If you trust in God and rest your mind on the fact that He cares for you and whatever concerns you, His peace will stand guard over all your thoughts and feelings. God's peace can do this far better than our human minds.

"You keep him in perfect peace whose mind is stayed on you, because he trusts in you. Trust in the Lord forever, for the Lord God is an everlasting rock (Isaiah 26:3-4 ESV)."

At this point, I think it makes sense for us to look at someone who inspired generations and continues to do so through the millennia. 'The Ten Commandments' and the story of Moses are a profound lesson for all those in quest of answers to their fears. From his days of youth in the Pharaoh's palace, when he had to face the harsh reality of his Hebrew lineage to relentlessly leading his people to the chosen land, against all odds, Moses is an inspiration for all those who wish to destroy their fears with the love of God.

As a Hebrew born in ancient Egypt, Moses was destined for a life in slavery. But it was destiny that led him to a royal life in the royal palace after he was rescued by the Pharaoh's daughter who found the little child in a wicker basket, floating on the Nile. On discovering his roots, Moses left Egypt and settled down to a mundane life in the desert. It is the first instance of Moses facing up to the uncertainties of life, when he could have easily sat on the truth and enjoyed a life of luxury till his death. I feel it was a situation where Moses faced his fears. But more was in store for him...for the next forty years at least! The next big moment occurs when God orders Moses to lead his people out of Egypt. This turned out to be another turning point in Moses' life, wherein he must return to Egypt and ask the Pharaoh to release thousands of slaves from bondage and allow them to leave the land of Egypt. Moses is beset by doubts and fears and tries his best to wriggle out of the situation.

Ultimately Moses understands that he is just a tool in God's hands and rises up to the challenges ahead. It is his faith and trust in God that leads Moses towards achieving his goals. The moral of the story is simple; believe and trust in God, and you shall achieve. In the journey to fight your fears, you will come across situations where God's presence will be vital. Remember He is there for you.

Together, you and I with God by our side, shall defeat our fears and walk the way to a life of peace and happiness.

KEY TAKEAWAYS

1. It makes sense to step up to your fears.

2. Regular and moderate physical exercise can be a good medicine for your fear issues.

3. Relaxation techniques are a good way to address the mental and physical characteristics of fear.

4. Jesus is the answer to all our fears.

Types of Fear

Most of the fears discussed so far are linked to danger. Running into a street is dangerous because a car may come and cause an accident, bringing pain and harm. Whether the danger is real, as with things that might hurt someone physically, or whether it is imagined, as with certain people groups being a perceived danger to society, most fears come from the desire to avoid pain. As ever, not all pain need be physical only.

Emotional pain also creates fear. A child whose father left home, may end up with a lifelong fear of abandonment. Someone who had their heart broken may fear entering another romantic relationship. This fear is still present because there's a perception that some sort of pain will occur, and if an action may cause pain, it's considered dangerous by the brain.

Often, fears are completely imagined. Because your brain is so efficient at protecting you, even if you think about things that might be dangerous or cause pain, your brain could react to that fear. Have you ever been waiting for someone to arrive at your home, but they were running late and were unreachable by phone? After a while, you probably started to worry that something bad has happened to them. Your brain imagines all the things that could be wrong and the pain that would come if the person had been injured. In minutes, you become afraid and worried, your heart racing and your palms sweaty, all because you imagined a scenario—which was completely untrue—that causes pain.

Since our brains are so efficient, there doesn't need to be real danger, for a person to feel afraid. The fears that come as a result of something learned or taught may cause a person's response to something that isn't always scary. A harmless spider, for example, would cause some people to have a physical reaction and become very afraid. Yet, the spider presents no actual danger. Through anxiety and worry, fear may be present over something that hasn't even happened or never will. These fears can be the most debilitating because they're governed by the brain's imagination rather than a clear and present danger. Your powerful brain is great at making up the worst scenarios, to keep you up all night with anxiety, causing you harm in the long run.

Closer home, when we get down to the actual practicalities of fear in our daily lives, the picture can be a daunting one. Phobia is the scientific terminology for fear, and it can manifest in our lives in one or more of the many types that are listed or not in medical texts. In fact, phobias have been acknowledged among the most prevalent mental illnesses in the United States. According to The National Institute of Mental Health, as many as 8% of U.S. adults deal with some type of phobia. Incidentally, women, more than men, are found to be more susceptible to experiencing phobia in some form or the other. As discussed earlier, phobias can be symptomized by signs such as nausea, trembling, speeding heartbeats, feelings of dislocated reality, and being fixated by the fear object.

As per the American Psychiatric Association (APA) fears or phobias can be listed under three broad categories:

- ▶ **SOCIAL PHOBIA** – is the fear of interacting with others and can adversely affect a person's professional, social and family relationships. Most people grappling with social phobia issues find it difficult to achieve their educational and professional goals. In extreme cases, people suffering from social phobia may become so reclusive as to avoid all social situations.

- ▶ **AGORAPHOBIA** - is a type of anxiety disorder symptomized by fear of places or situations that might make you feel trapped, helpless or embarrassed, resulting in panic. Typical situations include public transportation, open or enclosed spaces, standing in queues, or being stuck in a crowd.

- ▶ **SPECIFIC PHOBIA** - When a phobia is linked to the fear of a specific object, it is known as specific phobia. The cause could be anything from lizards to needles and water.

Psychiatrists have surmised that phobia triggers are categorized under four broad heads:

a. Natural Environment: Examples include astraphobia or the fear of lightning, hydrophobia or fear of water

b. Animals: Examples range from batrachophobia or fear of lizards to equinophobia translating to the fear of horses

c. Mutilations and Medical treatments: Examples such as hemophobia or the fear of blood, and trypanophobia meaning the fear of medical syringes

d. Situations: Claustrophobia or fear of closed spaces and aerophobia or fear of flying are typical instances of situational phobias or fears

The more discerning among us will realize that, like any other emotion, fear is information and provides us knowledge and understanding—should we decide to acknowledge and accept it.

Now, if we carefully sift through the layers and methodically unwrap the contours of fear, we'll end up realizing that only five basic fears provide the basis for the myriad phobias that control our lives and direction. These are:

▶ **Extinction**—is the first of the five fears and is concerned with the fear of annihilation, or the end of our existence. The very thought of no longer being around gives rise to a primary existential anxiety in normal people. Remember that scary feeling you feel in the pit of your stomach when you peep over the edge of a tall building.

▶ **Mutilation**—the prospect of losing a part or parts of our physical body can give the bravest among us the shivers. The fear of seeing our body's boundaries curtailed, or of losing an organ's functionality, body part, or its use in our daily lives is a traumatic sensation. The phobias aroused by the sight of insects and reptiles such as lizards, spiders, snakes, and other creatures, are basically caused by the inlying fear of mutilation.

- ▸ **Loss of Autonomy**–in other words, the fear of immobility, paralysis, restricted movement, getting enveloped or entrapped, feeling overwhelmed or smothered, being entrapped or imprisoned. This basic fear emanates from the panic of possibly ending up in the control of circumstances beyond your control. Scientifically identified as claustrophobia, this type of fear also influences social interactions and relationships.

- ▸ **Separation**–involves the fear of being abandoned, rejected, and the potential loss of connectedness; of becoming a person non grata–being unwanted, losing respect, or losing value of others. The typical "silent treatment," or social boycott that one experiences, usually by a group of people, can leave you devastated effect if you are the target.

- ▸ **Ego-death**–revolves around the fear of being humiliated or shamed, or any other process of intense self-disapproval that results in loss of self-integrity. Ego-death occurs when a person's imagined sense of worthiness is shattered. It seriously affects morale and capability of the affected person.

A close-up view of fear

When we set about to look out for fear in the daily humdrum, we'll find that most of the fears are usually centered around a few major domains – death, the unknown, failure, rejection, insufficiency, and man.

Looking at the domains listed above, several questions are bound to pop up in your mind. For example, why are we discussing only these domains. Some of you might wonder why are failure, rejection and insufficiency listed separately instead of being clubbed together. Similarly, there are many who feel death is inevitable, so why fear it? And then there are quite a few who find it difficult to understand the fear of man as a major stumbling block in our lives.

Interestingly, all of these domains – individually and in combinations thereof – are behind the fears that gnaw at the souls of millions of people across the world. As you read on, you will get to see the significance and impact that the fears arising from these domains, have on your life or that of your loved ones.

Let's face it, every person who is alive, will definitely ponder over what would happen when he or she is no longer alive: the fate of their family, their business, their wealth. So ingrained is our fear of death that we forgo of all the small pleasures in our anticipation of the day when we are no longer alive and kicking. Similarly, many of us get into a cold shiver at the prospect of facing the uncertainties of the unknown. And there are others who never venture out to do anything due to their fear of being rejected by others. A sense of insufficiency has been cited as the major cause behind the mental health problems of a significant percentage of people suffering from relationship issues. And finally, it is the fear of our fellow human beings, in terms of acceptance and approval, is something that we have all experienced at some point of the other in our lives.

Now, millions of people have overcome their fears by understanding the root causes, identifying the solutions, and finally applying the solutions in their daily lives. Needless to say, prayer and spiritual contemplation play a crucial role in recovery as fears are primarily mental processes that manifest in emotional and physical symptoms. That's why over the next few pages, I have carefully decoded each of these domains in detail. Going through each of these domains will equip you with the information and directions to rid your mind of the specific fears and live wholesome lives.

The following chapters outline each of the fear domains in detail, then go on to look at its manifestations, practical steps to tackle them and also the spiritual dimensions involved in a particular area of fear as seen from a Christian perspective.

As a practitioner and preacher of the Trinitarian Gospel, I strongly believe that the Holy Bible is a repository of useful knowledge that can resolve all our earthly troubles. Within its pages are the solutions for all our problems, and that includes remedies for our fears.

So, lets proceed without much ado to explore the major domains that instill fear in us...

KEY TAKEAWAYS

1. Like other emotions, fear is also information and provides us knowledge and understanding.

2. Most of the fears are centered around death, the unknown, failure, rejection, insufficiency, and man.

3. Prayer and spiritual contemplation play a crucial role in recovery

Fear of Death

As the phrase indicates, it is an anxiety that is triggered by the thought of death. It is also characterized by a feeling of something unpleasant occurring, the anxiety when confronted with the possibility of dying, or no longer 'being in existence'. There is also the morbid anxiety aroused by death-related thought-content, which can interfere significantly with our functioning in daily life. Lower levels of ego-integrity, increased physical ailments, and higher incidences of psychological problems point towards the presence of acute levels of death anxiety, particularly in those who are aged, considering their perceived proximity to death itself. But then, Jesus said ""Let not your heart be troubled; believe in God, believe also in Me", there's no need to be afraid. And Paul too said "The last enemy to be destroyed will be death". So, let's examine how Death need not be an issue anymore:

The scriptures tell us about a curse that was placed on a hanged person: "And if a man has committed a crime punishable by death and he is put to death, and you hang him on a tree, his body shall not remain all night on the tree, but you shall bury him the same day... Deuteronomy 21:22–23

In Jewish Law, most capital offenses had stoning as the form of punishment. Usually, the dead body would be hung in public to deter thoughts of crime in others. This law made it illegal to do so overnight (Leviticus 18:24–27; Numbers 35:3–34).

The apostle Paul referred to this law in relationship to Jesus and His death on the cross. In Galatians 3:13 we read, "Christ redeemed us from the curse of the law by becoming a curse for us—for it is written, 'Cursed is everyone who is hanged on a tree'". Jesus was cursed for us, hanging on the cross as a substitute for our sins. The law in the Mosaic economy was a precursor of Christ's redemptive work aimed at the human race's redemption.

Interestingly, the cross of Christ was often referred to as a 'tree' in Jewish contexts." Acts 5:30 states, "The God of our fathers raised Jesus, whom you killed by hanging him on a tree". Acts 10:39 says, "They put him to death by hanging him on a tree". See also Acts 13:29.

The broader narrative of Scripture shows us the relation between a tree and the idea of cursing and blessing. In Genesis 3 Eve and then Adam, eat the fruit of a forbidden a tree. In Revelation 22:14 the eternal state includes those who eat from the tree of life. A tree was involved in the entry of sin into humanity (through the tree in the Garden), the answer to sin for humanity (through the cross), and the ultimate removal of sin in eternity (through the tree of life).

As per the tenets of the Mosaic Law, those hanged on a tree were believed to be cursed people. As per the law, it was illegal to leave the body hanging overnight. The same law applied to Jesus too, who was executed on a tree, despite not committing any crime. The very day of his death by crucifixion, Jesus' body was recovered from the cross and buried. Intervening on our behalf, Jesus himself accepted the curse of sin, to redeem us forever from every link with the consequences of the fall of Adam, and its effects.

Thoughts on the fear of death at the age of 50+

The fear of death is by and large the preserve of those who are past their fifties. When the body is beginning to age and mind gets fatigued but responsibilities continue to stare you in the face, the fear of death grips us by the neck. It is at this stage of our lives that we are the most vulnerable to the thoughts of death and the resultant fear. So, how do we overcome this problem?

For a start, let's think logical. Look back at the journey past and the journey ahead, from a vantage point. Isn't it true that we have lived good lives so far? At this point, we should be able to look back and count our blessings. After all, we have created a community of friends, relatives and colleagues that stretch out more than 50 years. Most of us are excited about the many decades of life that we have ahead of us – decades that we want to fill with the passions, people and places that matter to us.

At the same time, as we reach our 50s, it's common to start worrying about our mortality. Many of us begin to think about the fact that we may have fewer years ahead of us than behind. Some may even come to fear death, no matter how far it is in the future.

Talking with the members of Sixty and Me, and Boomerly, I am always amazed how some people are afraid of death, while others find it easy to accept their mortality. So, to help those of you who have a fear of death, I asked them for their advice.

Here are a few tips, based on the advice of other people over 50 who have conquered their fear of dying. Here again I was struck by the fact that having faith in God, helped immeasurably in instilling confidence and casting away the fear of death. The majority of senior citizens who dipped into the Holy Bible for succor and strength, was both an eye-opener and heartwarming experience for me!

The first point my friends made emphatically was that you don't need to fear at all...

"So do not fear, for I am with you; do not be dismayed, for I am your God. I will strengthen you and help you; I will uphold you with my righteous right hand." Isaiah 41:10 KJV

"When I am afraid, I put my trust in you." Psalm 56:3

Always remember that it all starts by enjoying God as yours. Only then, you can spend quality time with the people you enjoy being around. Try new things, challenge yourself. Most of all, keep active and stay engaged with positive activities; "When anxiety was great within me, your consolation brought joy to my soul." Psalm 94:19.

Some of the other gems of wisdom that my life-hardened friends showered upon me included:

If there is something that really rankles you – pray about it! Prayer is another form of talking to God, confiding your hopes, aspirations, and fears in Him. Do your thing and leave the rest to God.

If you have unfinished business – take care of it in love! There's nothing worse than being left with incomplete tasks. So, never keep pending issues on the backburner. Do it today and do it with Love.

If you have someone you need to speak with – make that call! Time is a great healer but that's not a good enough reason to hold back if you want to speak to someone, who you're no longer close to. Relations are like plants. They dry up without water and nourishment but spring back to life the moment you nourish them. Relationships that dry up because you grew apart, can always be revived. All it needs is a phone call to get talking and before long, it'll feel like you were never out of touch in the first place!

Don't keep going to a job that is deeply dissatisfying, or stay in a relationship that makes you unhappy. You have many years to enjoy everything that life has to offer. Who you spend your time with matters; An anxious heart weighs a man down, but a kind word cheers him up. Proverbs 12:25!

The fear of death is often the fear of not living on your own terms. You deserve to see your dreams come true. The more you embrace life, the less frightened you will feel about giving it up when the time comes!

At this point, it makes sense to read a sentence that highlights the power of the word of God in our battle against the fear of death...

'The Power of Death was destroyed in the death of Jesus Christ' – a simple sentence but nevertheless the most powerful one that lays bare the shallowness of death in the face of Christ's love for us.

Let us go on to see how Paul looks at death: For if we believe that Jesus died and rose again, even so them also which sleep in Jesus will God bring with him.

Then those also who have fallen asleep in Christ ... 1 Corinthians 15:18 KJV

To me, the only important thing about living is Christ. And even death would be for my benefit. (Philippians 1:21 ERV).

You see, Paul already knew that Jesus died at His place and for that reason there was no need to be afraid of death again. Death died when Jesus died, what we experience today is simply leaving this body which was formed of dust; All go to the same place. All came from the dust and all return to the dust - (Ecclesiastes 3:20 KJV)

My way of understanding people leaving this physical body is simple. We were designed to enjoy God with God for eternity. The body we are using here can't remain forever for some of us. But there is the good news I want to share with some of us. There is a generation that will not sleep at all and will behold the beauty of our Lord and Savior at His full return from inside out.

Focus on living well

There are so many simple things that you can do to live a healthier and more positive life. In fact, sometimes the smallest steps, applied consistently, lead to the biggest changes. Make a commitment to walk every day, rain or shine. Explore your passions. Write a "bucket list" with all of the amazing things that you want to do. If you are busy living, you won't have time to worry about dying.

"Do you want to be counted wise, to build a reputation for wisdom? Here's what you do: Live well, live wisely, live humbly. It's the way you live, not the way you talk, that counts. Mean-spirited ambition isn't wisdom. Boasting that you are wise isn't wisdom. Twisting the truth to make yourselves sound wise isn't wisdom. It's the furthest thing from wisdom—it's animal cunning, devilish conniving. Whenever you're trying to look better than others or get the better of others, things fall apart and everyone ends up at the others' throats. Real wisdom is God's wisdom. The first step in the acquisition of wisdom is silence, the second is listening, the third is memory, the fourth is practice, and the fifth, teaching others. It is characterized by genuinely loving and getting along with others. It is gentle and reasonable, overflowing with mercy and blessings, not hot one day and cold the next, not two-faced. You can develop a healthy, robust community that lives right with God and enjoy its results only if you do the hard work of getting along with each other, treating each other with dignity and honor." James 3:13-18 The Message (MSG)

Plan for Your Passing on

Many of the questions that we have about dying are religious or philosophical in nature. But, what about the practical concerns? Many of us worry about dying because we wonder what will happen to our family after we are gone. Will our grandchildren be happy? Will our spouse be able to recover from our passing? If so, will they have enough money to continue to live the kind of life that they deserve?

These are all valid questions. The good news is that, while we can't control when or how we leave this world, we can control much of what we leave behind. Many people feel a sense of relief when they get their affairs in order - even if they have many decades of healthy life ahead of them. They know that, should the unexpected happen, their wishes will be clear and their legacy secure.

At the end of the day, the advice from other people over 50 who have conquered their fear of death is simple: focus on living authentically, passionately and well. A fear of death cannot take root in the heart of a person who is truly satisfied with their life.

"Have I not commanded you? Be strong and courageous. Do not be terrified; do not be discouraged, for the Lord your God will be with you wherever you go." Joshua 1:9

KEY TAKEAWAYS

1. The fear of death is by and large the preserve of those who are past their fifties.

2. The fear of death is often the fear of not living on your own terms.

3. If you are busy living, you won't have time to worry about dying

Fear of the Unknown

Fearing the unknown and worrying about it is a mental obstacle. It hampers your innate potential to give your best in all walks of life. Typically, whenever you come across any unfamiliar situation, you are filled with a fear that stops you from making the right decisions. People in such situations usually choose to escape rather than face the situation. As a result, such people end up losing out on the several opportunities that cross their paths constantly throughout their lives. That's why, many a times, we must be brave enough to step out of our comfort zone for a chance to achieve the good things that life has to offer us. Unfortunately, it is this very fear of the unknown that holds us back in our comfort zones.

If you are thinking 'wow, this is exactly what I'm going through and wish I knew how to handle this problem.', rest assured, you are not the only one to suffer thus. Fortunately, there are solutions available to address these types of fear. All you need to do is make some minor adjustments in your life and lifestyle.

The first step in the journey towards fearlessness of the unknown begins with educating yourself about what ails you and then face it rather than avoid it indefinitely. Fear of the unknown can manifest in your life via diverse sources. For some it could be a niggling worry over their new job while for others it could be fear of what tomorrow has in store. The covid-19 pandemic is perhaps one of the best examples to underline the uncertainty of life. Millions of people have suffered from sickness, loss of loved ones, jobs, income and security.

Step 1: Acknowledge your fears

Once you get to know your fears from close quarters, take a step back to understand how fear actually affects you. This will help you understand the roots of your fears of the unknown. Fear takes birth from certain situations we face, memories we have, or things. Now, diligently list out all those things that you fear, and those situations that you prefer to avoid in your daily life. Once you identify the specific fears and their underlying causes, you'll be better equipped to overcome them.

It is possible that our fears of the unknown are sometimes aroused by factors beyond our control. In such cases, conditioning ourself is the ideal way to curb the fear of such fears. For some, it could be an end to the world, while others may fear getting trapped in an elevator. Other may find such fears a bit dramatic as they are all beyond one's control. Educating ourselves about the actual risks in such situations can prove very useful for people suffering these kinds of fears. For instance, you would certainly feel better if the lift attendant assures you that 5 minutes is the maximum time that anyone has been trapped in the lift. Understanding the actual risks involved in any situation can assuage our fears to a large extent.

KEY TAKEAWAYS

1. Acknowledge your fears.

2. Understand the actual risks

Fear of Failure

Probably the most common problem that afflicts humans, fear of failure stops the bravest of us in our tracks. This is one fear than can literally defeat you before you even set out on achieving something. It is something akin to a rocket achieving escape velocity to leave the earth's gravitational pull to finally fly free in space. There are so many occasions in our lives, when scared of failure and the consequences, we don't even try out something.

The fear of failing can immobilize us to the extent that we do nothing – and end up as failures! As a result of our fears, we don't make progress in our life and end up losing out on what are potentially life changing opportunities.

Let's take a detailed look at the intricacies involved in the fear of failure – its meaning, the underlying reasons, the factors at play, and the solutions available – to enjoy life as God meant us to.

The genesis of the fear of failure

Before going to the causes of this fear, it makes sense to first understand the meaning of 'failure'. In This is because each of us has our own definition and interpretation of failure. Failure can mean different things to different people, depending upon individual standards, values, and belief systems. In effect, what you deem as failure could be considered a success for another person or vice versa.

Medically, fear of failure is known as "atychiphobia" or the condition where our fear is so strong as to prevent us from doing the things that lead us to our goals.

There are many probable causes that give birth to the 'Fear of Failure'. A typical reason for this kind of fear, is having critical or unsupportive parents. Children of such parents suffer humiliation in childhood and generally carry the burden of childhood negative feelings well into their adulthood.

Similarly, suffering a traumatic event can also trigger a fear of failure later on in life. For instance, if you had tripped on stage during a school play, it's possible that you could end up with stage fright as an adult. The childhood experience might have been so traumatic as to prevent you from enjoying the experience of performing on stage.

Experiencing Fear of Failure

Symptoms that indicate you possibly suffer from fear of failure include an aversion to experiment with new things or take up challenging assignments. Such people also indulge in self-sabotage behavior such as procrastination, suffer excessive anxiety, and in general a lack of enthusiasm to follow up on targets. People who fear of failure are also known to display a sense of low self-esteem or visible lack of self-confidence. They could also try to hide their fears under the garb of 'Perfectionism', by attempting only those things that they are confident of completing successfully.

Failure...Defined and Diagnosed

The Cambridge dictionary defines 'failure' as the fact of someone or something not succeeding. Other dictionaries also come up with roughly the same kind of explanation for the word. It can also be seen as the opposite or synonym of the word 'success'. So, something achieved is success and something not achieved, is failure.

However, we must also look at these words in the context of several caveats such as, all possible efforts have been made, the efforts so made have been earnest, situations were favorable, and so on. As we see, success and failure are dependent upon many factors and the slightest variation in any of these factors, or combinations thereof, can result in varying degrees of failure or success of any initiative.

In effect, when you set out to achieve something, the outcome could be a total success or achievement of entire objective or goal, or it could be partial success or achievement of some part of the objective or goal, or a total failure which means you couldn't achieve anything out of the efforts.

Now, it's time to take a closer look at the latter two scenarios – partial success/failure and total failure. Obviously when we fail partially or fully, there are lessons to be learnt from them. Lessons in the form of insights, ideas, connections, solutions, options that can potentially pave the way for success in other forms. And these lessons are the takeaways we get out of such 'failures'. It implies that, in absolute terms, there is no failure in anything that we set out to do!So, when there is no failure at all, why fear in the first place? Just go all out and attempt whatever it is you set out to do or achieve.

Moving on, my favorite definition of failure dates back to my school days, when we were taught that 'failures are stepping stones to success'. Life is simply not life, if a fair share of failures is not thrown in as part of the bargain. If you haven't failed in life, it's probably because you haven't really tried your hand at anything seriously enough. Remember the times when you learnt to ride a bicycle. It wasn't as if you just jumped onto the saddle and pedaled away. Initially, you would have fallen off the bicycle – a process that would have been common for at least a few days. Your body would end up getting bruised and ache through the nights. But then as the days pass, you learn to balance yourself on the bicycle and soon you find yourself pedaling away to glory. The moral of the lesson: No pain no glory; no failure, no victory.

Put simply, failure is not a defeat, rather it's a promise for the future. And therein lies the beauty of failure. The definition of failure lies within us. Failure can be the end of your dreams OR Failure can be the key to your future success.

History and modern times are replete with instances of men and women who sprang up from the ashes of failure, to emerge as shining examples of success. High school dropout Richard Branson went on to become the toast of the business world with enterprises under the 'Virgin' brand. You also have Bill Gates who left university to set up Microsoft. The next time hunger pangs hit you and you reach out for a bucket of juicy Kentucky Fried Chicken; remember you have old Colonel Sanders to thank for. At a time when most people his age were enjoying a retired life, the KFC founder was literally down to his last few dollars, walking the streets, urging people to sample his chicken recipe. He didn't give up despite repeated rejections until he got his first order. The rest, as they say is history. Talking of bygone days, we know how much King David did wrong, but God lifted Him higher.

The good thing is that every day, everywhere there are people like you and me who are confronting their fear of the unknown, scripting turnaround stories that would make the likes of Sir Branson and Col Sanders fill up with pride.

We can either look at failure as "the end" or we can try to unearth the success that failure usually cloaks. The next time you fail at something, try looking for the intended lesson instead of simply raising your hands and conceding defeat. Such lessons are important because they're measures of our evolution, showing us how we grow, preventing us from repeating the same mistakes.

Failure – the great teacher

Failures are also useful to help identify your hidden strengths; facets that you would normally ignore or be unaware of their existence. also teach us things about ourselves that we would never have learned of, in normal circumstances. Failure situations are also great occasions to discover who your true friends and well-wishers are.

How NOT to get trapped by the fear of failure?

Knowing how much God loves us and cares about us, is the simplest and easiest way to overcome our fears. It is these trying situations that highlight God's love for us. "On the contrary, in the thick of these things our triumph remains beyond dispute. His love has placed us above the reach of any onslaught... no threat whether it be in death or life; be it angelic beings, demon powers or political principles, nothing known to us at this time, or event in the unknown future; no dimension of any calculation in time or space, nor any device yet to be invented, has what it takes to separate us from the love God demonstrated in Christ. Jesus is our ultimate authority." Romans 8:37-39 MB

Remember that God is by your side and will never let failure befall you in anything that is honest and sincere on your part. Having said that, it's also important to note that there's always an element of uncertainty in everything that we do. But not reaching our goals or falling short in our outcomes is not reason enough to lose hope. Instead, face up to reality, explore opportunities, stay brave and persevere as long as it is appropriate. Ultimately, it's the experience that counts because of the lessons we learn from it.

Despite all the realities involved in the game of success and failure, there are certainly some options available for us to eliminate or reduce the fear of failing:

» Examine all possible outcomes – For many people, fear of the unknown is the seed behind fear of failure. Simply replace that fear by celebrating all of the potential blessings that Jesus Christ has freely blessed you with. "Even though I walk through the valley of the shadow of death, I will fear no evil, for you are with me; your rod and your staff, they comfort me." Psalm 23:4 KJV

» Learn to look positively at life – Positive thinking by appreciating God's goodness through Jesus, is a superlative way to build up on self-confidence while negating self-inflicted damage. "An anxious heart weighs a man down, but a kind word cheers him up." Proverbs 12:25 KJV

» Consider the worst-case scenario – Sometimes it so happens that the worst-case scenario may turn out to be genuinely disastrous. In such situations it is perfectly normal to fear failure. Fortunately for us, in most situations, the worst-case picture is actually not so bad as to cause us fear of failure. Recognizing and acknowledging this reality can be really useful in our fightback against fear of the unknown.

» Plan for a contingency – If you are afraid that you may not succeed at something, remember that we are all mere mortals who are but pawns acting out God's will. If it is not the Lord who builds a house, the builders are wasting their time. If it is not the Lord who watches over the city, the guards are wasting their time

(Psalms 127:1 KJV). With this tenet anchoring your heart, you will find abundance of confidence whenever you venture beyond your comfort zone.

Get out of the clutches of fear

In order to set goals, you need to first overcome your fear of failure. With fear on your mind, it will certainly be difficult to venture on any goals. And, as we know, setting up goals is a crucial activity because they help us chart our paths in life. Next time you feel afraid, just remember – no goals, no destination.

Visualization is one of the methods that experts consider a powerful tool to help set goals. Imagining how your life will be transformed for the better when you reach your goal can be a super motivation for moving forward in life.

On the flip side, visualization is a double-edged sword that can produce quite the opposite outcomes in people suffering from fear of failure. Studies have shown that people who tried visualization technique to dispel their fears of failure, often end up grappling with a strong negative mood.

But then, what could be the way forward?

There's a popular adage from my younger days that I keep handy for people who are afraid to take that first step towards a life free of fear... Little drops of water make a mighty ocean.

Begin by taking small steps in the form of a few, small goals. The initial or 'warm up' goals should be sufficiently challenging so as to encourage you rather than overwhelm you. These goals are your "early wins" that will help boost your confidence.

For example, if you are feeling too nervous to approach your department head to discuss an exciting new project which you're excited about, then make that your first goal. Stop by her office during the course of the week and talk animatedly about the topic and give her inputs on rolling the project.

Try to structure your goals into tiny steps that ultimately pave the way to bigger goals. At this stage, don't bother about the end picture; whether it's bagging a promotion, or graduating with an MBA. The trick is to take a step and immediately focus on achieving the next step. That's it.

Apart from building up your sense of confidence bit by bit, the 'one step at a time' strategy will encourage you to keep moving forward, while protecting you from getting overwhelmed by the prospects of the ultimate goal.

While discussing our journey to a life without fear, there are certain pointers to keep in mind...

Often, fear of failure could also be indicative of a more serious mental health condition. Negative thinking has been seen to have caused severe health problems and even death, in extreme cases. While the techniques discussed here are acknowledged to have a positive effect on reducing stress, it must be expressly understood that they are meant for guidance purposes only, and readers should take the advice of suitably qualified health professionals if they have any concerns over related illnesses or if negative thoughts are causing significant or persistent unhappiness. Health professionals should also be consulted before any major change in diet or levels of exercise.

... There are many who are afraid of failing, but that doesn't mean we must allow that fear to prevent our progress in life. Here are a few holy thoughts to shore up your sagging spirits in tough times:

"Brethren, I do not regard myself as having laid hold of it yet; but one thing I do: forgetting what lies behind and reaching forward to what lies ahead..." Philippians 3:13 KJV

Since, then, you have been raised with Christ, set your hearts on things above, where Christ is, seated at the right hand of God. Set your minds on things above, not on earthly things. - Colossians 3:1-2

Finally, brothers and sisters, whatever is true, whatever is noble, whatever is right, whatever is pure, whatever is lovely, whatever is admirable—if anything is excellent or praiseworthy—think about such things. - Philippians 4:8,

KEY TAKEAWAYS

1. Symptoms of fear of failure include an aversion to experiment or take up challenging assignments.

2. Often, fear of failure could also be indicative of a more serious mental health condition.

3. Knowing how much God loves us and cares about us, is the simplest and easiest way to overcome our fears.

Fear of Rejection

Rejection is an experience that almost every one of us experiences at some point or the other. It could take the form of being spurned by someone you love, or it could even manifest as failing to bag the dream job you had set your heart on. The fact is, rejection is such a common factor in our lives, that only people who avoid social contact or are recluses are probably not aware of what rejection is. But then it is quite possible that such people resort to a lonely existence precisely because they fear rejection! So, if you're a part and parcel of the society you live in, rest assured, you are a fair target for rejection. Fortunately, fear of rejection need not grow into a giant demon that stops you enjoying a fruitful life replete with healthy relationships with the people who surround your or come in contact with you.

Common Symptoms of Rejection Fear

The fear of being rejected creates a very damaging pattern of behavior in our lives. It can cause us to feel that we are not good enough and that we are a failure. Within relationships, it can cause us to become obsessive, clingy and jealous and can also destroy relationships that have barely begun through us becoming too serious too soon which can drive others away. This manifests itself whereby a partner simply having a chat with someone else can make us think that it's a sign that they're going to leave us or if we're separated for a short time from a friend or partner, we can sometimes feel anxious and even angry as we falsely believe that this means that they don't want to spend time with us.

Emotions fuel rejection fears

Interestingly, our thoughts are not responsible for our feelings of rejection. Actually, it's how we feel about ourselves that end up making us to feel rejected. Negative self-feelings are capable of triggering a plethora of other feelings, including that of rejection. Soon, before you even realize it, you start feel useless, lonely, humiliated, inadequate, pathetic, and a loser. The more we wallow in such emotions, it becomes even more painful to bear, making it harder to face potential 'rejection' situations because we are scared that we'll be exposed to such trauma every time in future too.

Why doesn't rejection trouble others?

Those who seem unfazed by rejection are basically very confident personalities who take rejection in their stride, well aware that it's part of the deal and needs to be confronted if one needs to progress in life. On a different plane, rejection is kind of growing up pain that is required for us to evolve spiritually, giving us courage to step outside our comfort zone. Instead of feeling bad or sorry for themselves, or taking it personally, such people rather they consider it a flaw or loss for the other person.

You too can overcome the fear of rejection

Say no when you don't want to say yes: People who fear rejection usually do so because they are mentally conditioned to trying to please others. If you belong to this category, the first thing you should be doing is say 'no' instead of 'yes' when you don't agree with something others say or do. By staying honest to yourself, you are in effect respecting yourself and thus raising your self-esteem and confidence. It's a good way to understand and appreciate occasions where people are likely to refuse or say 'no' if the situation were to be reversed.

Accept your plus points: Don't shy away from accepting compliments that come your way. Truth is, it's a good thing to celebrate your good traits that others notice and applaud. It's a great way to boost your confidence and be more open to facing rejection.

Visualize your fears and face them: Allow your mind to explore scenarios where you would likely be faced with rejection, and prod it to visualize a happy ending in which your wishes are fulfilled. This technique is effective to build self-confidence to replace the usual negativity that creeps in and leads to your worst fears coming true.

Now, let's see what advice the Bible offers for a life that's free from fear of rejection:

» The Lord will always take care of you, even in the face of rejection.

...My father and mother may abandon me, but the Lord will take care of me. – Psalm 27:10 (GNTD)

» The Lord loves you as his child.

...See how much the Father has loved us! His love is so great that we are called God's children—and so, in fact, we are. This is why the world does not know us: it has not known God. – 1 John 3:1 (GNTD)

Practical steps to freedom from fear of rejection...

1. You can start with a daily list of your goals and strategize on achieving them without getting sidetracked. The key lies in pleasing yourself and equalizing your energy levels by getting used to the idea of saying 'no' when you can't oblige others.

2. Keep mentally reinforcing yourself about your fundamental right to happiness. Don't allow feelings of self-worth be dictated by other people's acceptances or rejections. Instead of agonizing over a failed job interview, simply begin renewed efforts to pursue other vacancies or opportunities.

"For it is when the Lord thinks well of us that we are really approved, and not when we think well of ourselves." (2 Corinthians 10:18 TEV)

If fear of rejection is constantly preventing you from interacting with others, you are at risk of losing out on a host of wonderful benefits such as the happiness, warmth, fun and excitement that interacting with other people brings us. Remember, if you never find yourself in a situation where someone could tell you 'no', then you are also depriving yourself of the chance of receiving a 'yes' as an answer.

It's certainly an amazing thing to know that despite knowing every single thing about you, God continues to love you. The sum and substance are that no matter what happens and who rejects you, God will never reject you. The Bible says, "My father and mother may abandon me, but the Lord will take care of me" (Psalm 27:10 TEV).

KEY TAKEAWAYS

1. Rejection is kind of growing up pain that is required for us to evolve spiritually, giving us courage to step outside our comfort zone.

2. Say no when you don't want to say yes.

3. No matter what happens and whoever rejects you, God will never reject you.

Fear of Insufficiency

Do you ever get the feeling that, no matter what you do, there is never going to be enough? Not enough money, not enough time, not enough energy to accomplish the things you dream of accomplishing? Or never mind dreams—just enough energy to get through an average day would be appreciated.

Will I be able to pay my mortgage this month? Will I be able to go on that fun trip my friends are planning in a few months? What if my car breaks down and I can't afford the repairs? What if I run out of time and miss that deadline? What if that client never wants to work with me again? It's always straight to worst-case-scenario.

Sounds familiar? While the magnitude and scope might differ from person to person, most of us would identify with this kind of situation.

This is something I have dealt with sometimes, but then I realized that God is trying to set me free from that particular mode of thinking. Jesus teaches me through Paul the apostle: "...Nor do I mean that I have been in actual need, for I have learned to be content, whatever the circumstances may be. I know now how to live when things are difficult and I know how to live when things are prosperous. In general, and in particular, I have learned the secret of facing both - poverty and plenty. I am ready for anything through the strength of the one who lives within me." Philippians 4:13 (PHILLIPS)

Want more clarity on the fear of insufficiency?

Well, here is what the fear of "not enough" looks like in my life:

> » Anxiety around purchases or expenses—especially those unexpected or unnecessary ones.
> » Worrying about money or about how I will get things done.
> » Feeling frenzied during the day, running from one thing to the next.
> » Trying to fix things I don't know how to fix, or give gifts I don't have to give—because I am worried the need won't get

addressed if I don't meet it.

>> An inability to enjoy the things I do have because I'm focused on what I don't have.

>> Jealous feelings toward friends when they get something that I don't have

>> Competing and comparing, being really hard on myself for not "measuring up"

Perhaps for a long time, I just thought this is how everyone feels when it comes to money, time and energy. It is strange how something totally crazy can become "normal" when we live with it every day. It is not until you start to meet people who don't share your anxieties around "enough"–who seemed deeply content with themselves, their efforts in a given day, their income, their possessions–that I realized there was a better way.

And strangely, miraculously, these people actually appeared to have more–more time, more energy, more resources, with less effort–than anyone-.

What is a Scarcity Mindset?

Not in a million years would I have confided in you that I had a scarcity mindset. As far as I was concerned, I acknowledged and celebrated abundance in life. Growing up, a phrase that was repeated in my house, over and over again, was: God provides. And I would have repeated that phrase to you, even as an adult.

But the more I started to learn about a scarcity mindset and what it looked like, the more I realized this was something I too was struggling with.

A scarcity mindset, by my definition, is simply:

A persistent feeling of not having enough–feelings of inadequacy, fear of going without something, a lack of self-confidence–most often stemming from negative thought patterns around time, money and energy.

So, having a scarcity mindset has little to do with what you have in your bank account or how much time or energy you have to give in a day. It has very much to do with how we feel about ourselves and what we believe we can offer to this world.

Where Does A Scarcity Mindset Come From?

Our beliefs are most often fed by, and built around our experiences, and how we interpret those experiences—more so than what we are verbally taught. So, you can be told a hundred times, "God provides!" but if you are constantly struggling financially and don't have a good story to tell yourself about why you are struggling financially, it's easy for the unconscious story that forms to sound like this:

> » God provides—but not for me.

The other thing to remember is that you are immersed in a culture which thrives in convincing you that you are not enough. And when I say "thrives" I mean quite literally, thrives. Companies are literally profiting off of your feelings of inadequacy - that you are not pretty enough, not thin enough, not smart enough, not cool enough, not stylish enough, not fill-in-the-blank enough.

We must therefore reject the mindset that tells us there are only so many resources to go around. And, that in order to get what you need, you must fight for it, bargain for it, compete for it, and really only the smartest, savviest, hardest-working, luckiest people will "win" it.

A scarcity mindset sets us up for unhealthy competition, jealousy, anxiety, overworking, and confusion about what really matters most.

What is An Abundance Mindset?

There is something I have been practicing consistently over the past 14 years that seems to be helping me throughout anxiety surrounding money and time. So much so that I'm able to preach this Gospel freely in many nations and time. It's a small shift, but it has made a huge difference for me. I've seen tangible shifts in the resources available to me, yes.

But more importantly I have experienced a positive shift toward peace and soundness of the mind, even when I don't have exactly what I think I want or need. Why? Paul gives us an answer: "For we are God's handiwork, created in Christ Jesus to do good works, which God prepared in advance for us to do." Ephesians 2:10 KJV
We should not worry about what we have or don't have. Paul had to learn to live in the abundance and lack.

It's called an abundance mindset

An abundance mindset is, very simply, changing the story we tell ourselves surrounding our experiences of enough. It is taking the same desires, circumstances and experiences we have always had surrounding money, time and energy and changing the story we tell ourselves about it. Same experiences. Different story. Something like, the glass is half-full instead of half-empty.

> » When I get an unexpected bill in the mail, for example, I can say to myself, "ugh! Why does this always happen? I work so hard for my money and everyone is always trying to get a piece of it." Or, I can say to myself, "thank goodness I have the money to pay this bill. I am so provided for."

> » When someone asks me for time I don't really have to give, I can think, "Everyone always needs something from me. Why can't I just get an afternoon to myself?" Or I can say, "I wonder what it is about me that has such a hard time saying no. What am I afraid of?"

> » When it's a Saturday morning and I'm dreading getting out of bed because I'm out of energy, I can moan and complain and drag myself out of bed, or I can ask, "what would happen if I just slept for an hour longer? What if my to-do list isn't as pressing as I think it is?"

> » Where a scarcity mindset tells us there is not enough time to sleep in for another hour, or that our friend who asked for our time will be so lost without our help, or that everyone is always

trying to take our money from us, an abundance mindset simply says: life is complicated. There will always be competing needs and expectations.

We should realize that life becomes very complicated when we think we are the one making things to happen by our own abilities and strength. God does it all, "Let the beloved of the Lord rest secure in him, for he shields him all day long, and the one the Lord loves rests between his shoulders." Deuteronomy 33:12

Everything good comes from God. Every perfect gift is from him. These good gifts come down from the Father who made all the lights in the sky. But God never changes like the shadows from those lights. He is always the same. James 1:17 ERV

What is NOT an Abundance Mindset

To be clear, an abundance mindset isn't some "health and wealth" magic wand that is going to immediately transform you into a millionaire. An abundance mindset is all about receptivity.

In effect, it means I am open to receive whatever God ordained in advance for life. Here is the word of the Lord to Jeremiah: "I have good plans for you. I don't plan to hurt you. I plan to give you hope and a good future, Jeremiah 29:11 ERV

Feelings such as disappointment, confusion, pain, and so on are not what God planned for you before you. Happiness, peace and joy are not dependent on your circumstances in life, but they are the indicator that the Spirit of the Lord is at work within you (Galatians 5:22).

My happiness [Christ], I carry inside of me.

When you have true feelings of "enough" you can allow to flow into your life - what flows into your life and to flow out of your life what flows out of your life. you don't need to coerce or control people or things around you because you know that everything that happens to you is an opportunity to learn and that you will receive exactly what you need, exactly when you need it.

"My God will use his glorious riches to give you everything you need. He will do this through Christ Jesus." Philippians 4:19 ERV

Everything you need is already available to you, because of God.

That's an abundance mindset. And it's much easier said than done. By that I mean it's much easier to write about it than to actually carve out those thought pathways when you are facing loss, or a fear of loss, or a season of living without. Praise God for His abilities in us, "Tell everyone who is discouraged, be strong and don't be afraid! God is coming to your rescue..." Isaiah 35:4 ERV.

"...I am the Lord All-Powerful. So, don't depend on your own power or strength, but on my Spirit." Zechariah 4:6 CEV

Getting Over A Scarcity Mindset

"So, I beg you, brothers and sisters, because of the great mercy God has shown us, offer your lives as a living sacrifice to him, an offering that is only for God and pleasing to him. Considering what he has done, it is only right that you should worship him in this way. Don't change yourselves to be like the people of this world, but let God change you inside with a new way of thinking. Then you will be able to understand and accept what God wants for you. You will be able to know what is good and pleasing to him and what is perfect." Romans 12:1-2 ERV

One of the most important things we can do, I believe, to carve out these new stories for ourselves, is to deliberately change our thought patterns.

So, for example, over the past four years I have been allowing the mind of Christ in me to completely eradicate to root all of the negative thoughts I had (thoughts like, "no matter what I do, it's never enough!") and to replace those thoughts with the truth about who I am in Christ and what I have available as mine in Him, now!

KEY TAKEAWAYS

1. A scarcity mindset sets us up for unhealthy competition, jealousy, anxiety, overworking, and confusion about what really matters most.

2. An abundance mindset is all about receptivity.

3. Everything you need is already available to you, because of God.

Fear of Man

These two scenarios are merely like the tip of the proverbial iceberg. Whoever you are, wherever you are, whatever your personal, professional, social or cultural background, fear of what others think of you is a common problem. The only differentiators being situations and people. Nobody, including you and me, is inured from this fear. In simple terms it is nothing but the 'fear of man'.

Personally, I wish I could say that I have never dealt with this type of fear. But then honestly speaking, that wouldn't be the truth. Let me confess, the fear of man has been an unwelcome aspect of my life. But rather than wallow in the pain and uncertainty that this fear created in my life, I decided to tackle the bull by the horns.

The phrase "fear of man" is a biblical category of fear. It includes a broad range of preoccupations over what people think of us or what we do. At a fundamental level, there's nothing wrong if we care about what people think about us; nor is it is wrong to wish to be well thought of. Proverbs 22:1 says, A good name is to be chosen rather than great riches, and favor is better than silver or gold. A good reputation is actually a valuable thing to have.

The fear of man arises when we care too much about what people think of us. It is a two-sided feeling: on the one side it is an oversized craving for people's approval, and on the other, it is an oversized fear of people's rejection. Ultimately the fear of man pushes us to put people in the place of God in our lives, which is nothing but a form of idolatry.

I. The fear of man lays a snare

Proverbs 29 says the fear of man lays a snare. Here, the word 'snare' can mean the lure or bait that leads to a trap, or it can even refer to the trap itself. Snares, in the olden days, as they are today too, were devises –often nooses or nets – that were set out to capture animals or birds. Similarly, the fear of man ensnares and hinders us from living in the freedom that Christ has called us to. This fear restrains us from joyful living and doing good as long as we live; instead of the fickle pleasure of fleeting man. Interestingly, a big part of the effectiveness of a snare is that it is hidden.

How useless to spread a net in full view of all the birds! Proverbs. 1:17

The snare is hidden under leaves and brush so that the prey doesn't realize it is before it is too late. Similarly, the fear of man can be camouflaged in our lives, and in many different ways – it doesn't always look the same or catch us all on the same path. Whatever your personality or upbringing, there are ways that the fear of man can be sprung in your life if you are not watchful. Teens especially, I think you face the fear of man to a unique degree; it is called peer pressure. The pressure to think a certain way, talk a certain way, look a certain way, believe a certain way, like certain things, dislike certain things. Let us kick the brush and leaves aside and identify some of the ways that the fear of man can ensnare somebody, and then close by looking at the surprising answer to the fear of man in our lives.

a. The fear of appearing foolish

One of the most common ways the fear of man entraps us is by stopping us from doing something we know we should, or something that would be good for us, or something that would move us out of our comfort zone and stretch us - for fear of appearing foolish.

Many years ago, I wished to learn singing and so I joined a choir of the church where I discovered my already provided salvation in Christ. It was my first time; I used to sing myself but I wanted to really be good because I liked the way they were singing every Sunday. It really was not coming naturally to me. Singing all sorts of notes at the same time was natural to me. But doing it in all harmony and one tone wasn't. One of my Sisters, Epossi Monique, that I love dearly, was at the Choir with me. She was good and it was natural for her to just sing while I was struggling to just remain in one style. In short, I was all over the place. And there were quite a few times when I began to feel foolish. Actually, truth be told – I looked foolish the entire time! But there were times when I used to feel self-conscious about sounding funny among the most amazing voices surrounding mine. At one point early on, I was tempted to give up because the thought that I sounded funny began to creep into my head. I shook off the thought because I knew that I was a beginner and looked like a beginner. But for a few minutes I truly felt the power of the fear of man.

Now, that's one of the snares of the fear of man: some people live their lives boxed in a little cage called 'I won't risk looking foolish if I stay in these boundaries'. If you struggle with the fear of man in this form you know what I mean: maybe you don't take a class to learn something new because you might look foolish, or you don't reach out to new people because you might look foolish, or you don't use the gifts God has given you because you might look foolish, or you don't dance the chicken dance at weddings because you might look foolish...actually, you will look foolish! There are people who live in iron barred cages forged out of the fear of looking foolish – and they miss so many opportunities because they fear appearing foolish. My sincere advice at this point - Do not be one among them.

But what is even more serious is that the fear of looking foolish can silence us when the Spirit of the Lord is prompting us to tell someone how amazing Jesus is. 1 Corinthians 1:18 tells us that the message of the Cross is foolishness to those who are perishing. In other words, God didn't choose a cool way or a hip and trendy way to save us from our sin. Jesus dying on the cross seems uncool, weak, and foolish to the natural man. There's no way around looking foolish if we want to be faithful with the saving message of Christ being crucified. We must be prepared to look foolish for the sake of Christ as the fear of man not only entraps us, it entraps the message entrusted to us when we give in to it.

b. Trying to impress people

As we have seen, the fear of man, is a crafty snare and it's hidden from plain sight so that it can catch us by surprise. It would be a mistaken to think that this snare is only laid across the path of the timid, shy, and fearful kind of person. If you are the kind of person that looks them in the eyes and shakes their hand with confidence, takes charge when you walk into a room, are always the center of attention and the life of the party, the fear of man can ambush you on your path as well.

Often it hides under the leaves of trying to impress people - the craving to be admired, to be looked up to, to be applauded. The fear of man isn't as much a fear as it is a life centered around men – a life that is motivated by pride and how we appear in the eyes of others, so it can manifest itself in a drive to impress people. And the goal is the trap: we define our lives through the eyes of other people. We need to be the center of attention, we need to be liked, we need to be promoted, we need to be considered successful, because we think our lives and identities are determined by what people think, rather than what God thinks of us. Life ends up becoming a big performance and every day is opening night. We read the reviews to determine how we're doing. Such people may excel at what they do because they are driven by a fear of failure, or a fear of not impressing other people. Their identity is wrapped up in what others think of them, and it's a terrible cage. Sometimes the loud, gregarious kind of person, the one who always seems to be confident and in charge – can actually be masking a terribly insecure heart with all that bravado.

c. Trying to please people

Another common form of the fear of man, is when we are driven to please people. We hate to let people down. We hate to say "no" to people. We hate to have them not like us.

The remora, also known as the suckerfish, is a fish that attaches itself to other fish, to hitch a ride. We can opt to be human suckerfish, always sucking up to people, and always trying to suck up their approval. We want to leave a trail of people who are happy with us and we can't bear to think of people being unhappy with us. We become "nice" instead of "good" because "nice" doesn't ruffle feathers. We become chameleons who change with our surroundings. We tailor what we say depending upon who we're with, and we emphasize what we know they will agree with and stifle things we believe that they won't agree to. Pleasing people becomes more important than being truthful with them and faithful to God.

Paul wrote to the Galatians of this fear of man trap when he wrote, am I now seeking the approval of man, or of God? Or am I trying to please man? If I were still trying to please man, I would not be a servant of Christ. Galatians 1:10

Paul was not saying we shouldn't ever try to please people or that it's always wrong to want people to approve of us. He's talking about what drives us, what motivates us, what controls us. If our goal is to please people rather than please God, our service for Christ will be seriously hindered.

Again, the message of the gospel is an offense to those who are perishing, and if we are faithful to proclaim the gospel, it will offend some people. We shouldn't seek to be personally offensive – quite the opposite! – but if we are faithful to declare the gospel it will offend some people. And so, the fear of man will tempt us to tailor the offensive message of Christ into a nice and inoffensive message that doesn't risk offense but also doesn't carry the power of the gospel with it either.

These are just three common expressions of the fear of man. You might experience other ways the fear of man operates in your life. The important thing is to realize that it lays a snare – it will inevitably hinder you from doing what you are supposed to do and living in the good freedom of the gospel.

II. Overcoming the fear of man with God's help

The love of God is freely available for every single creature on the planet. This Agape-love is so overwhelming that it beautifies the lives of those who acknowledge and receive it. For those running away from it, it's like oppression of contradictions.

The fear of the lord comes from the Greek word theosébeia which is an expression of reverence and adoration towards God. You can't worship God if you don't love Him. Irrespective of how much you fear God, if there's no love in your heart then there's no God you can worship. Let your service to God be motivated by love and never by fear. Then I will repeat, do not dwell in the fear of God, but the Love of God. You will give Him your best when you are in love with Him. You will do only what you think is required if you relate with him based on the fear towards him - 1 Timothy 2:10.

Criticism is inevitable. It is the pastime of those who never achieve anything. If you seek to please men, it will be displeasing to God, and if God is not pleased, even the men you are claiming to please will be displeased with you at some point. But if you seek to please God, even to the point of displeasing men, God will cause the men that are displeased with you to become pleased with you.

The fear [agape-love] of the Lord is a fountain of life, that one may turn away from the snares of death. Proverbs 14:27

Focus on the fact that God has approved and qualified you, rather than looking at how you can be approved or accepted by people. To know that God has approved and qualified you is somewhat similar to the good cholesterol that prevents the bad cholesterol from building up in the arteries. Awareness of the Lord's approval of you is good for the heart and helps keep the fear of man from building up in our lives. Psalm 19:9 says the fear [reverence towards] of the Lord is clean – it cleanses and purifies our hearts of trash like the fear of man. The fear of the Lord puts life in proper perspective – God is big and the man we are afraid of, is small.

Scripture helps us to eradicate the fear of man and grow in the awareness of Jesus' presence

One of the ways we can educate our hearts in reverence towards the Lord and away from the fear of man is by memorizing scriptures that speaks of your freedom in Christ. I once attended a conference of a very popular minister of the Gospel in Africa. Before he started with his text of the night, he quoted Hebrews 13:6 (which quotes Psalm 118:6) So we can confidently say, "The Lord is my helper; I will not fear; what can man do to me?" I learned later that growing up, the pastor, I am talking about, had an overwhelming fear of speaking in front of people and one of the ways he learned to win over that fear was with scriptures. He was quoting that very scripture to still the fear of man in his own soul that evening.

There is a confession of the brave warrior King David that you can use whenever you feel like fear is holding you back. Psalm 27:1 - The Lord is my light and my salvation; whom shall I fear? The Lord is the stronghold of my life; of whom shall I be afraid?

David had a lot of people who hated him and wanted to take his life. But all that amounted to nothing because the Lord was his protector, the stronghold that kept and guarded his life. So, when we face the kind of fear of man, that paralyzes us, silences us, makes us afraid to step out or risk people's disapproval, we need to remember that only God is great and He holds our lives in His hands. Ask yourself - What can man do to me? Of whom shall I be afraid? The fear of the Lord leads us to trust in the Lord.

But what about that fear of man that has us craving acceptance, approval, even admiration? What about the kind of fear of man that doesn't experience like fear? Instead, it feels like a drive to be big in the eyes of men – to be looked at as successful, important? To be applauded and considered the best, the smartest, the most...you can fill in the blank.

The fact that God accepted you in Christ is enough to be at peace [Ephesians 1:4]. Because we begin to see that at the root of the fear of man is not only a small view of God and a big view of people, but, at a deeper level, a small view of God and a big view of ourselves. Pride is at the bottom of the fear of man. It's not that we care about others, we care about what others think of US! The fear of man is different than being others-minded in an unselfish, caring way. It's being others-minded in terms of what they can give us. Life becomes a giant negotiating table – we compliment them because we want their approval because we think their approval raises our stock.

KEY TAKEAWAYS

1. The fear of man arises when we care too much about what people think of us.

2. Criticism is inevitable. It is the pastime of those who never achieve anything.

3. The love of God is freely available for every single creature on the planet.

4. Scripture helps us to eradicate the fear of man and grow in the awareness of Jesus' presence.

5. The fear of the Lord puts life in proper perspective – God is big and man is small.

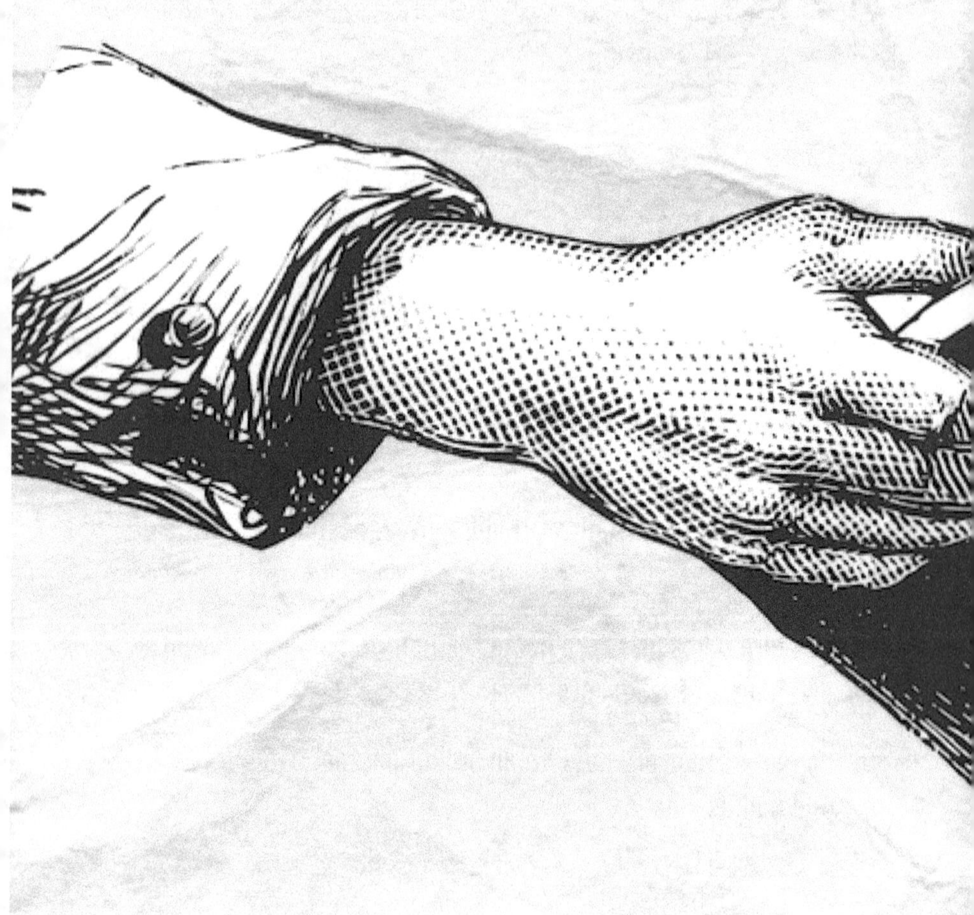

SECTION 2

Introduction

According to an old saying, more than the medicine, it is faith in the physician that cures a person. As someone who subscribes to this philosophy, I think it is in the fitness of things to replace the physician with God. Faith, it is said, can move mountains. So, what are a few fears that we encounter in our lives?

While the previous section examined the physiological and medical aspects of fear, in this section I have attempted to provide readers a focused look at the role of faith and spirituality in tackling fear.

Indeed, where there is no faith, there can be no victory. And, this is precisely where the power of faith and devotion to the Supreme Divine, come into play.

Over the next few pages, we look at the relationship between our life as human beings, fear, and God.

It's a fact that God, through Jesus Christ, has created us to live and love, and not to fear. I have systematically examined the subject from diverse perspectives and dimensions so that even lay persons can understand that God and His love stand firmly behind us so that we live our lives devoid of fear.

Together, lets unravel the distinctions between fear of God, His Love, and how to overcome our fear of Him...

The Relationship between God and man

Before we venture further into the realm of god and devotion, let's go back to a favorite childhood fable we all know. Yes, I have the tale of Androcles and the lion, in mind. It's a beautiful story that highlights the power of kindness and gratitude. Exactly the kind of relationship we enjoy with God.

In the tale set in ancient Rome, a Christian slave called Androcles escapes from his cruel master and flees to the forest. While wandering in the forest, he encounters a lion that is weak and moaning in pain. The kind-hearted slave examines the lion and discovers a huge thorn stuck in the lion's paw, removes the paw and treats the wounded paw. A few days later, Androcles is captured and sentenced to be thrown to the lions, as punishment. The huge crowd of spectators wait for the lion to devour Androcles in the arena. But to their utter dismay and surprise, the lion, evidently very hungry, simply walks up to Androcles and licks his face lovingly. It turns out that it is the same lion that Androcles had helped in the wilderness. The emperor orders the two to be set free.

Interestingly, kindness and gratitude, are the two qualities that are highlighted in this evergreen story of Christian piety. If we look deeper into the story, we can see that our relationship with God is based on His kindness and our gratitude.

We Are Not Meant to Live in Fear

When God first created us, He never meant us to be afraid or anxious. God is Love by nature, which implies that we were made by love. Remember, we are in His image and after His likeness [Ecclesiastes 3:14 records that 'what God does is FOREVER; nothing can take away or add unto it']

Adam forgot who he was in the eyes of God as soon as he partook in the tree of the knowledge of Good and Evil. Rather than focusing on the goodness and kindness of God, he replaced all the great moments they had with the fact that he was naked, unworthy or not good enough to stand in the present of God just how he was prior to the apple. This is the problem most of us have today around the world, we agree to the fact that God is love but on the back of our heard we don't actually understand what that means, so we are never free enough to feel His embrace in our lives. Some of us are concerned about being alienated, separated, or becoming enemies of God as soon as we do something, we think can change His opinion or mood towards us. The reality is that, it is all in OUR MINDS, just as it was for Adam. God still came to Adam like nothing ever happened but Adam couldn't feel fellowship with God; not because God changed, but because Adam's view of God and himself changed since he opened up to corruption. According to Paul's letter to the Colossians 1:21. You were God's enemies in YOUR mind, not His.

There's absolutely no fear in Love, just as there's no absolute death in Life. Adam was never afraid before he partook to the wrong tree. God never intend for us to be afraid of him, nor of anything else He created; instead, everything He created has always been for you and I to have fun and behold His face through it all while on earth. The phrase "fear the Lord" is often misunderstood as saying that we should be scared of Him or tremble when we are in His presence, but this is the total opposite of what God always desired. God wants you to feel more at home in His presence than what you could possibly feel when you are around your biological parents. The word "fear" used by Paul the apostle is actually the Greek word phoibe which means radiant. Jesus made the invisible God visible to everything created. He is the radiance of God's beauty. We can't be one day motivated by fear and another day by love. Many times, in the scriptures, when an angel appeared before someone, the person was usually told not to fear, before the angel went on to deliver the intended message.

God made us to be in communion with Him, to have a relationship and be in harmony with Him, to enjoy His creation and experience love and peace. Under the law of Moses, certain actions were prescribed for the people of Jews to be protected from "God's anger". While animal sacrifice covered their sins temporarily, following the ten Commandments was the only way to "appease God".

When Jesus came to earth, all of that changed. Jesus gave up his own life so that we could have a living relationship with His Father; this was never meant to be a relationship based on us doing the right thing but on the power of His work to free us to the uttermost. God has gifted us grace and peace through Jesus Christ our Lord. The Bible says that where fear is, there is no love: "There is no fear in love, but perfect love casts out fear. For fear has to do with punishment, and whoever fears has not been perfected in love (1 John 4:18 ESV)." This one verse makes it clear that things have changed since Moses' day. In our generation today, everything created shouldn't be motivated by any form of fear in his relationship with God or any other being. Where there is fear, there is terror, fright, panic, distress, dread, worry and anxiety. On the other hand, wherever there is love, there intimacy, devotion, adoration, worship, deep affection, tenderness, warmth, endearment, acceptance, enjoyment and fondness. The relationship most people had with Yahweh in the Old testament was one motivated by fear, which portrays a very unhealthy relationship.

Now, we understand that we were all in the same boat; our distorted behavior is the proof of a lost blueprint. While the Old testament Law proved our dilemma, the grace of God announced our redemption in Jesus Christ. In the eyes of God, we are innocent; not because we are perfect but because His love for us speaks louder than our distorted behavior. God is the one who made us righteous, not ourselves—Paul the apostle tells us in 2 Corinthians 5:21 that Jesus became sin so that we [all men and women] may become the righteousness of God once and for all. The gift-principle puts the idea of been rewarded based on what we "do" or "don't do" obsolete. So, if God made us free from the power of darkness and brought us into the kingdom of His Son, then there is no longer a place for fear in our lives. God's love is the ultimate antidote to any fear you can be experiencing in your life. Any area in your life where fear still rules is precisely an area where you trust Him the least; there, we likely find our greatest fears. This alone is a reason for fear to be overcome. Otherwise, the Bible would not repeatedly assure us to "fear not."

You should embrace the fact that we live in a broken world and we will all experience a mixture of good and bad. No amount of fear will change that mix. But, knowing that you are loved, accepted by God and that you have been blessed and highly favored will develop your internal strength and resolve to tackle any situation with your head held high.

If God is love, which the Bible tells us in 1 John 4:8, and there is no fear present in Him, then the more of God/Love is experienced, the less afraid you become. Since we know He made us to be in a relationship with Him, experiencing His love in all we do, we know that He does not want us to live in any form or shape of fear. When we truly know who God is and trust in Him, we experience freedom, peace, joy, and happiness. There will be no stress and worry in the places that we trust God. This doesn't mean we will not face challenges, we all do but they will not dictate our mood, break us or distort our attitude, but as the scripture says in Romans 8:28 We know that in everything God works for the good of those who love him. The desire of any parent is to see their kids be the best at whatever they do or will do in life, so is the desire of God regarding all of us. He loves us much more than we can imagine, He wants us to be aware of that beyond the shadow of a doubt so that we can be the best versions of ourselves and live a life free of fear.

The feeling of fear is probably one of the strongest emotions we experience. Nothing else can so completely overwhelm a person. No other emotion lingers in the body for so long. However, there happens to be something stronger than fear, and that is Love/ God. Love is the most potent force on the planet. So powerful, that it can effortlessly wipe out even the strongest fears that plague us.

As we can see from the above discussions, our struggles with the emotion called fear, can only succeed when it is based on love and trust in God. So, go ahead, take firm steps to welcome God into your life and see your fears evaporate away. Belief in God, is the biggest positive factor that adds strength to all the physical and practical aspects involved in facing our fears.

As it has been so famously said, Faith can move mountains!

Ultimately, it is your faith in the true God, that will stand by you through the trials and tribulations of resolving your fears, and living a wholesome life.

Drive away your fears and revel in the love of God. Nothing can touch you when you have God in your heart.

KEY TAKEAWAYS

1. When God first created us, He never meant us to be afraid or anxious.

2. There's absolutely no fear in Love, just as there's no absolute death in Life.

3. Embrace the fact that we live in a broken world and we will all experience a mixture of good and bad.

A Comparison of Fear and Devotion

While it's easy to understand terms such as fear, love, devotion, trust in isolation, the problem arises when we look at them with relation to God. Invariably, we turn to the scripture, only to find ourselves further muddled by the wealth of knowledge and information compiled in those books. The lack of awareness or the inability to understand available literature on the topic leads to confusion, misinformation, and possibly disbelief. To resolve exactly such issues, I have taken up the topic in detail here. Once we are finished with this chapter, you should be able to see these emotions from a higher perspective. The objective here is to bring you closer to God, in your search for solutions to banishing fear from your life.

The Fear of God

If God is love and love drives out all sorts of fears, then why do some translations of the Bible or some religious leaders, repeatedly tell us to fear God? It certainly seems like a great contradiction, and if you do read these passages with a literal definition of the word "fear", you could get confused. The proper meaning of the word fear used in the scriptures has its origins in the Greek word yiraw whose meaning tends more towards showing reverence and honest recognition. Throughout the Bible, especially in the Old Testament, we come across many verses mentioning the fear of God or fear of the Lord. In other translations/versions, the word for fear is translated as honor, awe, or worship. Love should be the factor that causes us to worship and honor God for who He is, rather than fear.

We have been included in a relationship with God for a journey of romance with Him. But that would remain impossible to enjoy if our devotion to Him is motivated by fear. How can we ever love God if we fear He will retaliate against us? If there is no fear in love, then there is no way to both love the Lord and fear the Lord at the same time.

"Long ago, at many times and in many ways, God spoke to our fathers by the prophets, but in these last days he has spoken to us by his son, whom he appointed the heir of all things, through whom also he created the world (Hebrews 1:1-2)."

In the Old Testament there was an even greater misunderstanding of who God is than there is in the world today. Our ancestors did not have the Holy Spirit permanently by their side, to guide them and bring them into truth. Before Jesus, only prophets could periodically hear from God, but today, anyone who believes Jesus is the Son of God and sees that He is Lord, has the Holy Spirit living inside them. The primary ministry of the Holy Spirit in us is to help us understand who Jesus really is, and Jesus always reveals His Father.

It's tempting to read the Bible and thinking that the God in the Old Testament is different from Jesus in the New Testament. But we know that God is the same today as He was from the beginning. Jesus is the word according to John; He is the same yesterday and today and forever (Hebrews 13:8).

As the scriptures tell us in John 1:1, "In the beginning was the Word, and the Word was with God, and the Word was God," then we know that God didn't suddenly have a change of heart when the books that constitute the New Testament were written. He has never been against us but for us. His nature has always been one of perfect love, and it will always be.

It's easier to understand God when we look at Jesus. It is only because Jesus is fully God, and was also fully man, that we are able to relate to Him on a more human level. By relating to Jesus, we relate with the Father as well. Jesus himself said in John 14:9: "Have I been so long time with you, and yet you haven't known me yet, Philip? he that hath seen me hath seen the Father; and how can you say then, Shew us the Father?" And then, he also said in John 10:30: "my Father and I are one." Even the prophets and priests who were originally the only people who could hear from God, still did not have an understanding of His nature, because the way Jesus revealed the Father to be, was very different from what they knew God to be. They saw the punishments being poured out throughout the Old testament, but most couldn't interpret the language of God due to the fact that they didn't have the Holy Spirit. We see how astonished everyone was when Jesus walked on earth. No one expected the relationship with God to be easy and based on nothing else than Love alone. This influence of the old traditions didn't stop after Jesus came, and became what they were, in order for the human race to become what He has always been to the Father. In 1741 Jonathan Edwards gave a sermon on "Sinners in the Hands of an Angry God", which is one of the most influential sermons in the Christian world's theology today. This sermon contributed to create the conviction in people's awareness that God isn't happy but angry and that He is always ready to destroy or kill whenever we fall or make a mistake. But that certainly isn't the truth about who God is and what He is all about. Everything you need to know about God [Father, Son and Holy Spirit] is displayed in the most accurate way through the person and work of Jesus Christ, the Anointed One. That is why, whenever we look at Jesus, it's so easy to see God as Love itself.

Jesus never rejected anyone, nor made anyone feel afraid or unworthy of Him. He also never made anyone feel afraid of His Father in heaven. Everyone who met Jesus while he was on earth was able to see and experience the true nature of God - that of a loving, caring Father. Jesus made it very clear that He did not desire anyone to feel afraid, in John 14:27: "Peace I leave with you; my peace I give to you. Not as the world gives do I give to you. Let not your hearts be troubled, neither let them be afraid." If you want to experience the peace that passes understanding, you have to give up your right to understand everything.

As you can see, the fear of God is a misplaced one and God actually loves us for all our inadequacies and weaknesses. The thing to do would be to set aside your doubts in this regard, and surrender yourself to the unlimited love and joy that Jesus offers you. Through these pages, I have made a humble attempt to untangle the confusions of incomplete information, semi-truths, and misconceptions, that prevent you from allowing the life of Christ to express itself through you, and a solution to the fears that gnaw away at your happiness. Welcome to a fearless world as nothing now stands between you and God.

KEY TAKEAWAYS

1. Love should be the factor that causes us to worship and honor God for who He is, rather than fear.

2. It's easier to understand God when we look at Jesus.

3. Jesus never rejected anyone, nor made anyone feel afraid or unworthy of Him.

For the Doubting Thomas in You

Despite all the explanations, it is possible that there are a few who need some more assurance to take that amazing leap of faith – from doubt to trust and love. It is perfectly understandable because all of us are unique – in terms of physical, mental, emotional values. For the more stubborn among God's children, being able to overcome their inhibitions may certainly be more difficult. But it's not an impossible task. In fact, such people are the ones who immerse themselves completely in the Lord's love, once their doubts are dispelled. I have worked on this section, precisely for such people. Nothing gives me greater joy than strengthening their belief in the core principles of the Christian faith.

Overcoming our fear of God

Despite all the scriptures on love and the many verses that tell us not to be afraid, some people may still fear God. If there is no personal revelation of God's love in your heart, there will be no authentic trust in Him. Since faith pleases God, a lack of faith and the presence of fear hinders our relationship with Him in many ways.

Being afraid of God shows our misunderstanding of who He truly is. The presence of fear in your heart indicates a lack of persuasion of His love and care for you, and everything else that concerns your life. For example, if you are afraid of going to the doctor to have tests run, then you're not trusting God that everything will come out okay. If you are constantly terrified of being in a car accident, you are not trusting God who loves you, because if He loves you then he will protect you. On the other hand, when you acknowledge that you died when Jesus died and rose with him as Paul said in Ephesians 2:6, then you will say just as Paul said in Philippians 1:21-23 "To me… even death will be for my benefit; to leave this life is to be with Christ." When you have faith in that, you are not afraid of death. List all the areas you often feel afraid of, close your eyes and think about how God loves and cares about you, then allow the peace that comes from that conviction to settle in, then see how the lies of enemy in those areas will dissolve. When you have an accurate understanding and authentic experience of God's love, fear can no longer hold you captive nor control you.

In a way, having fear in a particular area actually hinders you from seeing the hand of God in that area. Love is essential for grace to work His miracles through faith. So, if we fear, we are not trusting Him to take care of the situation.

We often act on our fears in an attempt to prevent or change the situation we are facing. If you are afraid that you won't have enough money to pay your bills, that fear may cause a number of things to happen. You might pay bills with a credit card, which makes your overall financial situation worse. You might find yourself unable to sleep because of the worry, and that lack of sleep may lead to a lesser performance at work, which could lead to less money in the long run. Trusting God that the money will be there, will help avoid the more damaging actions that might come from trying to fix the situation on your own.

If God really wanted us to be afraid of Him, His nature could not be one of love since love casts out fear. Love and fear cannot exist together, so if God is love, He cannot be fear, nor will He accept anything coming from it. The prophets of the Old Testament shared with us what they thought was beneficial for us to know. Those who spoke about fearing God, said so according to the dispensation there were living under. If God wanted us to be afraid of Him, we could not genuinely and freely love Him. And the Bible clearly tells us that He loves us and I believe once we understand that, His love leads us to respond to Him effortlessly. He does not want us to be afraid because He wants a close relationship with us, and no one can genuinely love and trust a person they are afraid of.

This truth is also reflected in the life of Jesus. On earth, He was a very loving person. He did not try to make people afraid of Him, rather He told them not to fear. Jesus could not have both been scary enough for us to fear Him and caring enough for us to love Him. Jesus showed us the Father's love and His grace. The Holy Spirit living inside us gives us the revelation of this love in both understanding and living.

According to 1 Corinthians 13:4-7, God/Love is patient, kind, does not envy or brag, is not arrogant or rude, does not demand its own way, is not irritable or resentful, does not rejoice in wrongdoing. But He does rejoice at the truth, bears all things, believes all things, hopes all things, endures all things. These verses may have become so familiar to you that you don't think about the definition of love very hard. If we consider each of the elements that love is, and compare it to the life that Jesus lived, it's easy to see how He personified love in every way.

During the times when Jesus had to correct someone, He did so to their benefit - in a way that would make them aware of the fact that they are better in nature than whatever the distorted behaviors they were struggling in. Even in anger, He did not act with resentment or irritability, did not become arrogant or rude, and did not demand that things be done His way. He acted only on what the Father told Him to do and speak.

The Trinity of God is a community in itself, and a perfect example of love in the way each person of the godhead relates to the others. This is again easiest to see in Jesus since He was the word who become human, just like you and I. In all that Jesus did, He obeyed His Father. When He didn't know what to do or say, He waited for the Holy Spirit to guide Him. When Jesus shared our fears so that we could be healed from them, he was afraid of going to the cross and asked God to take the responsibility of it from Him, He still obeyed the Father and went to the cross as us, though He was so stressed about doing it that He sweated blood. If Jesus can have faith in His Father during His darkest moment when He was facing the most terrible circumstance any person could face, then so should we. This is what God wants for us, to live by the faith of the Son of God, we should trust Him in all areas of our lives, in all matters, big or small.

When we fully trust in God, there is no more room for doubt or insecurity. Instead, there is only peace and kindness, understanding and truth, endurance and hope. God does not want us to be afraid of anything because it keeps us from knowing the greatness of His love and it keeps us from achieving greater things in life. Eliminating fear makes more room for confidence and assurance, which in turn brings us peace that allows us to be our true self. God did not create us to have a life full of anxiety and worry. He created us to love and be loved.

KEY TAKEAWAYS

1. Being afraid of God shows our misunderstanding of who He truly is.

2. We often act on our fears in an attempt to prevent or change the situation we are facing.

3. When we fully trust in God, there is no more room for doubt or insecurity.

SECTION 3

Introduction

We have reached that stage where we have our basics and practicalities about fears, firmly in place. However, before you actually set out to implement the takeaways, I feel it's my responsibility to acquaint the reader further with the realms of God's Kingdom.

It's perfectly understandable that during the course of our journey, we sometimes lose steam and are in danger of giving up the war against fear. Anticipating precisely such situations, I have included the following chapters to revive your enthusiasm and renew your confidence in the Lord's love.

More than body and mind, addressing our shortcomings requires application of spirit. This is where most people fail to sustain their initial enthusiasm and soon let go off the benefits derived from understanding the factors and implementing the steps given here.

I believe that the spiritual connect between us - humans, and God, is vital for the success of any initiative that we venture upon. Over the next few chapters, we look at the issue of fear at a higher plane.

For one, acquiring greater clarity on the spiritual aspects of fear will go a long way in strengthening emotional strength and also contribute to the physical and mental well-being of a person. More importantly, it contributes to consolidating on the reserves of spiritual strength that were developed through the readings so far.

Ultimately, it's only our participation in the faith of the Son of God that can sustain our journey in life and the battles we fight throughout. Follow these thoughts and implement them in mind, body, and spirit to see your fears dissolve over time

The Consequences of Fear

The very first time we come across the concept of fear in the Bible, is in the Garden of Eden. God created Adam and Eve, the first couple, given perfect paradise to live in innocence and enjoy. They had a close relationship with God, and it began with no consciousness of separation, delay or sin. Despite their close relationship with God, they allowed enough of doubt to creep into their minds so that it caused them to fear.

A look at the story of creation shows us that everything started out just fine. God made Adam, then decided he needed a partner, and created Eve for him. The couple were placed in the Garden of Eden, and given authority over all the creatures of the earth. They had plenty of food and enjoyed a great relationship with God. So, what went wrong? Fear came into the picture and spoiled the entire show.

It all began when Satan, the liar, successfully captured the attention of Eve in the garden. He used his greatest attribute which is to lie to ruin Adam and Eve's relationship with God. It was Satan's lie who first put doubt into the min of Eve:

"He said to the woman, 'Did God actually say, 'You shall not eat of any tree in the garden'?' (Genesis 3:1-3 ESV)."

These words show us how the devil leads the woman to question what God said. He simply twists the words around and changes the very meaning of what God instructed the first couple to do. When we carefully see what God actually said in Genesis 2:16-17, it's quite clear: "And the Lord God commanded the man, saying, 'You may surely eat of every tree of the garden, but of the tree of the knowledge of good and evil you shall not eat, for in the day that you eat of it you shall surely die.' (ESV)."

Satan twisted things around so craftily that Eve was forced to say no. God had expressly said that Adam and Eve could eat of any tree they liked except one, whereas the serpent asked if God told them not to eat the fruit of any tree at all. The serpent's question contained some truth and some untruth, leading to ambiguity. But Eve corrected him and repeated what God had said. However, she added that merely touching the tree would cause death, even though God had only said that eating its fruit would cause death. By this time, she may have been acting out of fear already. If she was afraid that the serpent would try to trick her, she might likely exaggerate and twist God's words to prove that no, He did not say what the serpent claimed. It only goes on to get worse from there onwards as we can see today.

The serpent continued his lies, claiming that what God said wasn't actually true: "But the serpent said to the woman, 'You will not surely die. For God knows that when you eat of it your eyes will be opened, and you will be like God, knowing good and evil.' (Genesis 3:4-5 ESV)." We can't possibly know what Eve was thinking when she heard this, but we certainly know, through her subsequent actions, that she started to question herself on why God made it clear to avoid eating from that specific tree.

Now, imagine yourself in a similar scenario. Your boss tells you to complete a project quickly or there will be a consequence—if the deadline is missed, the client will become angry. As a result, you start to work your hardest, clocking long hours of overtime, to do your best because you like and respect your boss. Then, a coworker comes in and asks if you'll be fired if you don't complete the project. Well, no, you think, he didn't say that at all, he only said that the client would be mad if the deadline was missed. Perhaps, in your eagerness to show you know what the boss said and that your coworker is wrong, you add in that the boss had warned that the client might go elsewhere if the deadline is missed. At that point, it merely seems like a possible outcome, after all.

And then your coworker drops a bomb on you. He tells you that the deadline isn't really the day you thought it was; that your boss wants you to work hard only to make him look good. The coworker goes on to mention the bonus that the client is offering if the work is completed early, and says that the boss would pocket it all for himself. If you're a hard worker and know your boss well, you might recognize right away that this isn't true. Your boss wouldn't ask you to work overtime and make a tight deadline if he alone was going to reap the rewards. Maybe you go on doing your work, thinking your coworker must be mistaken.

But by now, the seed of that thought has been implanted in you.

The thought buzzes around your head even as you're working. You're spending long hours away from your family, away from the things you love—it seems that you're being punished in some way. Now that you start to think about it, you wonder if maybe the boss is just using you to get ahead after all. Maybe he's hiding the real reward—the bonus from the client. Then your coworker drives in the final nail. He suggests that if you give the work to the client yourself, you could be the one to receive the bonus, not your boss.

In that moment, it takes a lot of trust to continue working and not think badly of your boss. Most people would question the situation and demand to have a talk with their boss. It's in our human nature, after all. If it wasn't in us to question, then Eve wouldn't have ever questioned the serpent. But, she did.

In our present-day scenario, if you listen to your coworker, you'd have to go behind your boss' back to give the work to the client. Of course, your boss would be upset. But the fear of being used overrides the desire to please your boss. You might fear that you won't be recognized for doing the work. You might fear that there is a bonus you'll miss out on. You might fear that you'll have to keep working overtime to please your boss when actually, it's not crucial that you work so much and it's only for his personal benefit. Anyone in your place would probably want to avoid a similar situation. You'd have to really trust your boss and know that he wouldn't ask you to do something unimportant or beyond your capabilities. You'd really have to have the faith that you'd be rewarded for going above and beyond.

Unfortunately, Eve was not enough grounded in the knowledge God shared with Adam. She feared or suspected that God was keeping something from Adam and her. She worried that she was missing out on being more powerful, on knowing more, and on being more like God. She feared that somehow, not having this knowledge would harm her. She acted on her fear and partook to the lie of the devil. Adam followed her lead, even knowing that the serpent was possibly lying. He too partook as well, because even with his suspicion of the serpent, his fear of not having that knowledge was greater.

The story doesn't end there. Adam and Eve quickly realized they'd done something wrong. God showed up as usually, and they feared again: "And they heard the sound of the Lord God walking in the garden in the cool of the day, and the man and his wife hid themselves from the presence of the Lord God among the trees of the garden" (Genesis 3:8 ESV).

They distanced themselves from God by hiding from Him. Instead of admitting what they'd done, they tried to hide in their fear. They were likely afraid of how God would react. Maybe they thought they'd be punished or that they would die a natural death. Maybe they didn't know what to expect at all at that point; and that fear alone was enough to keep them hidden away. They felt shame at being naked and fear of God's reaction in that moment, and they acted on their fear by fleeing.

In this crucially important story of the history of everything created, we see that a simple fear led to a massive outcome. Fortunately, not all of us will cause all of humanity to fall if we act against what God said, but the effect on our individual lives can be just as catastrophic. While there was an overall consequence for the whole of humanity—that we believed a lie about God and about ourselves—Adam and Eve also faced personal consequences, and those consequences were immediate.

Right after Eve feared, she ate the fruit she was not meant to eat. This caused her husband to also disobey God's direct advice. Then their fear increased. They hid, therefore created distance and delay between them and God. They also felt shame. Within moments of the serpent showing up, Adam and Eve both went from enjoying paradise to living in fear and shame, being further from God than they'd ever been. But it didn't stop there.

Once God found them and came to address the issue, things got worse.

Adam turned on Eve when he was questioned, saying, "The woman whom you gave to be with me, she gave me fruit of the tree, and I ate" (Genesis 3:12). Eve, in turn, blamed the serpent, claiming she didn't know better and that she'd been tricked: "The serpent deceived me, and I ate" (Genesis 3:13). Now, in addition to the separation they created between them and God, there was separation between husband and wife. Neither took responsibility for what they'd done, and instead, they tried to point the fault to someone else, fearing that they would face a terrible consequence otherwise. Fear had now caused division within the marriage as well as their spiritual lives.

The consequences for their sin, came along next. Eve and all women were told about the greater pain in childbirth, and the struggle of wanting to please their husbands. Adam was informed about the pain and trouble in getting food from the ground, causing harder work to be required of men. The final consequence was that the couple was removed from the garden. They lost the luxury of living in paradise, and their relationship with God, and with each other was damaged. All, being the result of acting on fear.

We may never know the way things would have transpired if Adam and Eve had trusted in God fully instead of fearing him. They may have continued to stay in Eden, enjoying the closest relationship with God imaginable, for the rest of their lives. Perhaps their children would have learned from them and would have also lived in the Garden of Eden for all of their days. We can't know for sure, but we can see the outcome that came from their fear and know that it would have been better if that fear had not been present or acted on.

KEY TAKEAWAYS

1. When fear comes into the picture, it can spoil the entire show.

2. A simple fear can lead to a massive outcome.

3. Fear can cause division within the marriage as well as their spiritual lives.

Fear forces us to live out of a mistaken Identity

If we don't know the true nature of God, we don't know our own true nature - since we are made in His image and likeness. Without a proper understanding of who we are in Him, it's easy to not only fear, but to have an incorrect view of our identities.

Without a proper knowledge of who God is, you might go about your life doing what you think are good things, living in a way you believe to be good. Yet, something is missing. You don't know what it is. So, you search for something to fill its place. Some turn to drugs or alcohol, some to sex and gambling, some to overeating or anything that attempts to fill "the hole". No matter what you try, nothing quite brings the satisfaction you're looking for. As a result, you keep on looking out, trying harder to fill "the hole" that grows larger, within you, every day.

Until one day you meet someone who seems to be different. This person has everything you want—a good life, also real peace and joy, happiness and success, and an uncanny ability to bounce back and not let anything get him down. You ask him about his life and try to figure out why he's different from you. Maybe he's just hiding the empty feeling. Maybe he's found a better way to fill "the hole".

In talking to him, you discover that he never seems to be afraid of anything. He talks about God and all the things He's done for him; all the ways in which his life is great because of who God is. Maybe you don't know God at all or maybe you've been going to church your whole life but haven't seen the results your new friend seems to have. Where your life is filled with worry and anxiety, he sits back and relaxes, saying that God already handled it and everything will work out in the end.

As you get to know him, you find that he talks about God not like some distant beings in the sky, but as a community of beings he personally knows and loves; they're real and alive, and he has a deep, connected relationship with. He talks about God's love and how he never has to fear because of it. He talks about being His child and all that comes with being a member of the family of God.

Over time, you begin to see the difference between you and your friend. What you believe about God doesn't seem to match what he believes. Where he has complete trust, you still worry. Where he knows God loves him, you doubt. Something is different in his relationship with God than yours. It comes down to what we believe about God's nature.

You may fear that God won't come through for you when you're applying for a new job. You may fear that your children will go down a bad path in life and that God won't keep them from getting involved in harmful things. You may fear that the pain in your back will get worse and doubt God's ability to heal you.

All of this fear comes from what you believe about God, and by extension, yourself. If you believe that God will help you get a new job, that He'll keep your children from harm's way, and that He will heal your pain, then you can see Him as a loving and caring Father, giving His children all the love and attention, they deserve. If you have nothing but fear, you'll see God as stingy and uncaring, either not powerful or withholding blessings from you. In essence, the way we see God influences the way we see ourselves because we are made in His likeness.

When we have the wrong view of ourselves, it hinders faith. If we don't believe God can heal us, then we'll believe we're destined to be sick and in pain forever. If we don't believe God loves us, we'll believe that we're not worthy of love and will avoid relationships because they could bring pain. If we don't believe that God can help us overcome, then we'll believe we're stuck in our addiction or hopeless state and that we're worthless.

When we apply the power of the Gospel and understand God's Word when it teaches us His true nature, the picture looks very different. If we believe in the healing that God provided to us in Christ, then we'll experience healing. It will make us feel alive and fill us with hope. If we believe that God loves us, then we'll love ourselves and be ready to give that love to someone else. If we believe that God can deliver us from a hopeless state, then this alone gives us hope and we can look at our lives and know that things will improve and we'll not be stuck forever in despair.

Understanding God's true nature helps us see ourselves better and helps us be conscious of His unchanging love for us rather than fear Him. We cannot continue to put our trust in ourselves or our anxiety and expect to have a good life. We have to get to know God as a Father with a deeply loving, caring nature before we can feel worthy of that love and see ourselves as people who reflect His love and live, in peace. Putting faith in fear causes us to see God as a strict Father who withholds good things, who doesn't give love or affection. This leads us to feel worthless, unlovable, and keeps us in a place of hopelessness.

When we know God loves us and cares for us, that He has our best interests in mind and has the power to bring good things to us, we'll see ourselves as worthy of that love and those good things. And this fills us with hope, peace, and joy. It leads us to accomplish the things we're trying to achieve without the fear holding us back or getting in our way.

KEY TAKEAWAYS

1. If we don't know the true nature of God, we don't know our own true nature.

2. When we have the wrong view of ourselves, it hinders faith.

3. If we have faith in the healing God provided to us in Christ, then we'll experience healing.

4. When we know God loves us and cares for us, it leads us to accomplish the things we're trying to achieve without the fear holding us back or getting in our way.

Made for Love

Because we were born from above, God gave us His Spirit. According to 2 Timothy 1:7, "God has not given us a spirit of fear, but of power and of love and of a sound mind (NKJV)." Our relationship with Him cannot be based on fear. He loved us before we were even aware of what love was (1 John 4:19).

A slave may fear his master. If the master is difficult to work for, gives frequent punishment, and makes unreasonable demands, the slave will not love his master. The slave will fear or despise his master, or end up doing both. He may do the work to avoid being beaten or punished. He may act from a place of fear of his master. This does not lead them into a loving relationship. Given the chance, the slave who fears his master won't hesitate to leave and be free of him forever.

God made us free. We are not His slaves, but His children. There is a great different between being someone's child and being their servant. We are called to fellowship with Him in Christ and love one another. And we willingly do so – not from a place of fear or to avoid punishment. We are in fellowship with Him and can love Him because He first loved us. Think of your own family or friends. Those you love will get more of your time and energy. You'll be willing to do things for them that you wouldn't do for someone you have no relationship with. Many times, we're serving our family and loved ones. We do it because we love them, not because they are forcefully demanding us to do so.

In a similar situation, if a wife is being abused by her husband, she might start to see herself as a being of lesser value, then will start to serve him, not out of love. She somehow is nothing more than a servant in many ways, falling under his heavy hand when she doesn't do what he wants. There is no relationship in this kind of marriage if she is forced to do whatever her husband demands even if it goes against who she is. She does it because she's afraid of being hurt or being left alone. She does not act in love rather in fear, and again, if she was given the chance, she would gladly get out of the bad situation. Even if she never leaves, a husband who abuses his wife can never expect to have a quality marriage relationship.

God always wanted a Father, to son or daughter relationship with you. You're a part of His family - not as slave nor as servant but as a beloved son or daughter. He wants us to love each other so much that we choose to serve each other with our time and actions. We do this out of love, which builds a closer relationship. In order for us to continue growing in our consciousness regarding our union with God, there must be a ceaseless awakening to love. Fear will only hinder us, keep us away from God in our own mind, and make us act from a place of fear rather than out of desire to honor from a place of love.

God calls us children and has made us His own. Most parents would not want their children to be afraid of them but to love them back, and God does not want us to be afraid of Him. Most parents would want to enjoy a close and free relationship with their children, and for them to obey out of love, not fear. Similarly, God also wants the same thing. We are His children and He knows what is best for us as the ultimate Father. If we fear Him, we may not see the love behind something He asks of us. Fearing Him takes us out of close relationship and makes us servants who serve, bowing down to a hard task master rather than willingly giving ourselves as son and daughter to our dear and loving Father.

If we take a closer look at the verse in 2 Timothy, there is more there than just not having a spirit of fear. Not only do we not have a spirit of fear, but we have a spirit of love, power, and a sound mind. These three elements—love, power, and a sound mind—can all work together to set us free from fear forever. When Paul wrote this letter to Timothy telling him what sort of spirit he has, it was because Paul wanted Timothy to understand fully what was inside him. There is nothing timid about the spirit living in us, and we should be so in tune with that spirit, so aware of the integrity of God's word, that we can fully trust Him, He blessed us with the faith of His Son so that we never fear again.

This verse shows us the key to overcoming not only fear, rejection, feeling not good enough and many other things we deal with in life. When we have a mind that is set free through the spirit of love, we become unstoppable. Fear will no longer rule us or hinder us.

Fear keeps us in bondage. It takes us away from all that God is to us, away from the source of our power and peace. It takes us closer to everything we are afraid of - a place where everything reeks of darkness. By steeping us in fear, the enemy can accomplish much through us. We will act according to our fears, which is to align ourselves with the kingdom of darkness, rather than acting from our true self, which is who we really are when we align ourselves with what God believe about us. When we align ourselves with the one who wants to destroy us, we're stepping further away from who we really are. All the benefits of being children of God—peace and joy—are gone when we give in to our fears and remain there. Faith, peace and love take us back to God, and away from fear.

When we are convinced of God's everlasting love for us, when we know that His love is unconditional and that we are accepted by Him, then we have the security we need to enjoy having a sound mind. The more we understand God's love, the less we will worry and the more sound our minds will be. His love brings such peace that if we can get to the place where we live in His love, we will be unshakable.

Then, should things ever go wrong in life, we will be the ones standing tall, able to face whatever comes our way. We will be able to cast mountains into the sea instead of staring up at them, trembling in fear. When everyone around us is afraid and has doubts, we will experience a sublime peace that will hold us from giving up. Living in fear shows that you haven't received a full assurance of God's love for you. Once you are convinced, you won't have to fear anything ever again.

KEY TAKEAWAYS

1. God made us free.

2. God calls us children and has made us His own.

3. Fear keeps us in bondage.

4. The more we understand God's love, the less we will worry and the more sound our minds will be.

Taking the Leap from Fear to Love

By now, you are probably waking up to the importance of believing in God's love and trusting Him. Yet, if you have picked up this book and continue to read, it must be for a reason. Somewhere in your life, there is doubt on His love or His ability to take care of you and your situation. You may have been living in fear for a few weeks or a few years. You might be so far from God in your own mind that you doubt He even likes you, let alone loves you unconditionally. If you've gotten into this place of fear, it's not too late. God never turned His back on you. He will not abandon you to your fear.

Let's read the parable in Luke 15:11-24:

And he said, "There was a man who had two sons. And the younger of them said to his father, 'Father, give me the share of property that is coming to me.' And he divided his property between them. Not many days later, the younger son gathered all he had and took a journey into a far country, and there he squandered his property in reckless living. And when he had spent everything, a severe famine arose in that country, and he began to be in need. So, he went and hired himself out to one of the citizens of that country, who sent him into his fields to feed pigs. And he was longing to be fed with the pods that the pigs ate, and no one gave him anything.

"But when he came to himself, he said, 'How many of my father's hired servants have more than enough bread, but I perish here with hunger! I will arise and go to my father, and I will say to him, 'Father, I have sinned against heaven and before you. I am no longer worthy to be called your son. Treat me as one of your hired servants.'" And he arose and came to his father. But while he was still a long way off, his father saw him and felt compassion, and ran and embraced him and kissed him. And the son said to him, 'Father, I have sinned against heaven and before you. I am no longer worthy to be called your son.' But the father said to his servants, 'Bring quickly the best robe, and put it on him, and put a ring on his hand, and shoes on his feet. And bring the fattened calf and kill it, and let us eat and celebrate. For this my son was dead, and is alive again; he was lost, and is found.' And they began to celebrate.

Jesus told this parable so that we could learn something of the Father's nature. He is always watching for His lost child to return. He is waiting with arms wide open, ready to bring you back into His love, so you can realize that your relationship with Him hasn't changed in His mind like it has in yours. It is possible to find your way if you have lost everything and don't know what to do or how to go back to Him. It is possible to return to where you belong. No one can be called lost unless they belonged in the first place. He is our Father from the very beginning and we were made is His image and likeness. He remains faithful even when we are not (2 Timothy 2:13). It is not too late to come running back to Him.

KEY TAKEAWAYS

1. God never turned His back on you.

2. He will not abandon you to your fear.

3. It is not too late to come running back to Him.

True Faith

God certainly did not give us the spirit of fear. You might know this to be true. You might believe that He loves you and you may even be able to recite scripture verses that talk about God's love. Yet, the truth present deep down in our hearts, only surfaces when it's tested. It's one thing to say you trust God, but another to act on that trust when confronted with a scary situation.

We're told to pay close attention to what is in our hearts, to what we're really believing: "Keep your heart with all vigilance, for from it flow the springs of life" (Proverbs 4:23). Guarding our hearts with "all vigilance" implies a deep level of watchfulness. This isn't something we should think about once and a while. We should be constantly checking our hearts, seeing what's going in and out, and what remains there. If the springs of our lives dry up or become tainted, every area of our lives will get affected.

There's enough good reason for us to give careful attention to what's in our hearts. Whatever is in our hearts is the truth of what we believe- good or bad- and that's what will come out in our lives: "The good person out of the good treasure of the heart produces good, and the evil person out of evil treasure produces evil; for it is out of the abundance of the heart that the mouth speaks" (Luke 6:45). We may give the impression of doing good and, therefore, having good in our hearts, but our words and actions only go so far, and they can't fool God: "All deeds are right in the sight of the doer, but the Lord weighs the heart" (Proverbs 21:2). He knows what we believe in our hearts, but what matters most to Him is what He believes about us.

Just because things aren't going well in our lives, doesn't mean that God has failed us. He promises to never leave us or give up on us (Hebrews 13:5). When something unexpected happens, it is not an indication that God's character has changed or that He's somehow abandoned us. When faced with a scary situation, it is not the time to doubt or question God. This is the time to keep trusting, despite what the circumstances seem like.

What does it actually mean to believe in God? The original Greek word is *pistis*, in Greek mythology, to have faith in God is a practical commitment—the kind involved in trusting God, or, trusting in God. (The root meaning of the Greek *pistis*, 'faith', is 'trust'.) This, then, is a fiducial model —a model of faith as trust, understood not simply as an affective state of confidence, but as an action. This concept applies whether we are convinced in our minds of positive or negative things. When we focus on a problem and fear rises in our hearts, we convince ourselves that only bad will come of the situation. We are actually able to energize our fear, living the moment as though the projected outcome already happened. When we focus on God's Word, peace and hope come, and usually along with them, a better outcome.

It's easy to confuse whatever you want or hope for, with positive thinking or positive words. Most people rely upon positive thinking and positive words to demonstrate their faith. This is actually the new age system of operation. The amazing difference between the Faith of Jesus in which we are partakers today, and "the faith" we manufacture to obtain things by thinking and visualizing them is that the Faith in Christ doesn't wait for something to happen in the future. This is because everything has been given, provided and done by God in Christ. On the other hand, we have the positive thinking or positive words which are the mode of reaching out to the man-made gods, to give us things we want. There's nothing that we are expecting tomorrow, because Paul the apostle tells us that everything is ours right now and He also says that we have been blessed already (1 Corinthians 3:21-23; Ephesians 1:3). Thinking or speaking positive are not equal to trusting in God (knowing that what He said is true). Just because we think and say the right things, certainly doesn't mean that fear isn't ruling us deep down inside. It doesn't mean we're not feeling fear or trying to cover it up. All it means is that we've managed to think and say something positive. This alone is not faith. While Faith celebrates what grace has provided, positive thinking and positive words are simply equal to attempts to satisfy what we recognize to be absent in our lives, right now.

Real faith is not only present in what we think or say, but it's what already lives deep in our hearts and drives our lives. A person acting on the faith of the Son of God will not pace the floor, waiting for the doctor to call with test results. Instead, he or she will thank God in prayer because everything works out for good somehow (Romans 8:28). A person who placed his trust in Jesus when it comes to paying off a debt will not only think and speak accordingly, but will also not feel stress every time the bill comes and the balance still looks high. Faith does not waiver, but positive thinking and speaking do because they're not anchored in the faith in our hearts.

Faith is not limited to faith in God, however. We can just as easily put faith in our own mistakes, trusting that we will mess up. We exercise faith towards what people call "Murphy's Law," the idea that if something bad can happen, it will happen. We put faith in doctors instead of the God who healed us by the stripes of Jesus Christ. We put faith in our paychecks instead of the God who blessed us with everything and provided for us everything we could ever have needed. We can put faith in anything we choose to convince our minds of. Once our minds are convinced of something, our actions, thoughts, and words will follow.

This is why fear is so dangerous. It not only invades our minds, but our entire beings. It takes the place of faith in God since fear and love cannot exist in the same space. We can't have faith in love and fear at the same time. We must choose to put our full trust in one or the other. We can't have both of them.

KEY TAKEAWAYS

1. God certainly did not give us the spirit of fear.

2. We can't have faith in love and fear at the same time. We must choose to put our full trust in one or the other.

3. Real faith is not only present in what we think or say, but it's what already lives deep in our hearts and drives our lives.

Final Words

We finally reach the end of our journey of discovery into the world of our fears. Together, we have discovered the vast gamut of the emotion that can be scary and impede our enjoyment of life as God meant it.

For me, personally, it has been a meaningful experience, unravelling the diverse facets and layers of fear as we set out to demystify and resolve the problems that fear has brought into our lives.

I'm confident that by now, you would have successfully overcome your fears about fear, and made the transition from a life beset by worry and doubts, to one filled with joy, confidence, and anticipation of the opportunities that life brings your way in the shape of challenges.

Henceforth, you'll find that your entire outlook is one of hope, faith and trust. Hope – for a fear-free life, and a happy life unfettered by uncertainty and worry. Faith – in God. Trust – in His love for you.

I wish you success in your life ahead, confident in the belief that as you follow the tips, and stay steadfast to the words of God, every day will be one filled with happiness, kindness and human values that make our world a better place.

YOU ARE BLESSED!

Acknowledgements

All my years of engaging masses in the conversation of the ages (the gospel) have given me the privilege of connecting directly and indirectly with so many people, and I acknowledge all of you, because you have shown me what the material of this book needed to express: the importance of your unique experiences and the importance of you. You have helped me understand the need for helping people crush their fears and become who they're meant to be.

To my precious family – I acknowledge your endless love, support and prayers... there is nothing like it!

Mrs Puppala, my research assistant, you truly are an amazing support, I acknowledge both our hours of discussions about this book and your outstanding and honest editing. It is a pleasure working with you.

Christ In All Nations' Team: Once again, I have been thrilled and extremely blessed by your professional and loving support. You are my family, you guys play such a huge role in making my work accessible to so many in such an excellent way. Thank you, Paul Young author of The Shack, Dr. Baxter Kruger author of The Shack Revisited, Prophetess Beth Thomas, Doumbe Endene Marie, Shadrack and Anne Kiunga, Chantal Reymond, Yvan, Eudes, Simon and the rest of the team at CIAN: You guys are truly amazing, I acknowledge you and thank you

The Ultimate Confession

Pray this prayer:

"Dear Father, in the freedom of Your endless love and in the safety of Your divine embrace, I acknowledge that Jesus Christ is Your eternal Son. I got lost in my own darkness, instead of living in Your joy. I got crippled inside, instead of receiving Your love; my soul was disturbed.

Today, I acknowledge and believe that the life of Jesus from His birth to His seating at the right hand of God was vicarious. I was co-crucified with Jesus; I co-died on the cross with Him; I was co-buried together with Him; on the third day I co-raised from among the dead with Him; I co-ascended on high with Jesus and I am co-seated at Your right hand with Him. I acknowledge in my heart and agree to the fact that Jesus Christ is Lord of all and overall.

I give myself in love to You today, just as You gave Yourself in love for me and to me. Here I am Father, Jesus, and Holy Spirit, LOVE me. Amen."

If you sincerely repeated these words, welcome back to your real senses.

The Father God welcomes you and celebrates your return [**return to the consciousness of your true identity**]. You are a partaker of the saving work and life of Jesus Christ. The journey of love and discovery has started.

It is important for you to continuously grow in the knowledge of the love, the person and finished work of Jesus Christ by allowing your soul to be fed with the words of grace. For you have been crucified with Christ, it is no longer you who live, but Christ lives in you. Therefore, the terms co-crucified and alive together with Christ defines you now. Christ in you and you in Him. It is a blessing to know that the life you live is entirely by the faith of another (Jesus Christ), so you have nothing to worry about from now on. He got your back from start to finish. Live your life overwhelmed by God's opinion of you.

I advise you to find a Christo-centric local church to learn more about Jesus, His Father and Holy Spirit, then you will discover who you really are and what already belongs to you by virtue of your origin and identity. Celebrate who you already are in God's family every single day of your life.

You matter to God!

I invite you to share with us the wonderful things God did in and through you while and after reading this book. We would love to hear your reviews and feedback. You can also purchase additional copies of Freedom From Fears to give away to those you care about.

For more information about booking the author to speak to your organization or group, please contact Christ In All Nations Inc at info@christinallnations.org.

If you enjoyed this book, here are some ideas to help you share this book with others:

» Give the book to friends, even strangers, as a gift. They are not just getting a compelling, page-turner, but also a magnificent glimpse into the true nature of God that is not often presented in cultures around the globe today.

» If you have a website or blog, consider sharing a bit about the book and how it touched your life. Do not give away the plot but recommend that they read it as well.

» Write a book review for your local paper, favourite magazine or website you frequent. Ask your favourite radio show or podcast to have the author on as a guest. Media people often give more consideration to the requests of their listeners than the press releases of publicists.

» If you own a shop, business or you are pastoring a church, consider putting a display of these books on your counter to resell to customers. We make books available at a discounted rate for resale. For individuals, we offer volume discount pricing for orders of five books or more.

» Buy a set of books as gifts to battered women's shelters, prisons, rehabilitation homes, and the like where people might be really encouraged by these prayers.

» Talk about the book on e-mail lists you are on, forums you frequent, and other places you engage other people on the internet. Share how this book impacted your life and offer people the link to the amazon book page.

For more information about Alain Lea, please visit: www.christinallnations.org

About the author

For more than a decade, Alain Lea has been criss-crossing the world, spreading the Truth of the Gospel. His profound revelation is known for its clarity even while it retains the original simplicity of the Trinitarian Gospel. As the Director of Christ in All Nations, Apostle Lea has trained several ministers of the Gospel, in the United States of America and around the globe. His students are spread across America and different parts of the world, taking the good word of the Lord to millions of people yearning for the revelation of the sons of God. A prolific author, Alain Lea has written numerous books, including "Freedom From Fears" and "Heart To Heart". His mastery over the Gospel, coupled with his understanding of the physical and emotional aspects of sufferings, have led him to pen books on diverse subjects. During the course of his long years in the service to the Lord and mankind, Alain Lea has produced an extensive collection of teaching materials – in print, audio, and video formats. His ministry is actively distributing free audio tapes and CDs to all the needy people who yearn for God's Love. Alain Lea can be contacted at:

dralainlea@christinallnations.org

Or

Christ in All Nations Inc.
P.O Box 588
Granger, IN 46530

CONNECT WITH

Apostle Alain Lea

For more information, visit:

Facebook
@dralainlea

Instagram
@alainlea

Available on Amazon

The Void

In a world were religion seems to grow increasingly irrelevant, THE VOID wrestles with the timeless question: Where is God when He is needed the most? The answers will astound you and perhaps transform you. You will want everyone you know to read this book!

Christian was the only son his parents had, but both died before he had the chance to know them. He grew up with friends who became part of his life for many years. They all had very tragic stories to tell and were all experiencing a Void within that none of them could explain. After years of trying different things and ways to live a better life, they always ended up in more pain and trouble than before. In the midst of their greatest confusion, something very mysterious happened to one of them and left the others extremely suspicious. Apparently, God opened the eyes of Christian to the source of fulfilment. His life was gradually a reflection of pure beauty, with vision and purpose.

Now he is tasked with the mandate to reach his eight closest friends who have not known the freedom of living without the Void. They are in danger of being consumed and destroyed. He knows his window of opportunity is small because he has a vision of one of his friends dying, but he doesn't know which one.

What Now?
Once Lost Now Saved

It is so easy to forget what faith is all about. We struggle so much, work so hard, and fail so often that we frequently sense something in the equation of life must be missing.

Alain Lea argues that what we are missing is the gospel in a fuller, more powerful understanding of Jesus and what His finished work means for everyday life.

During his adolescence, Alain Lea discovered the power of the gospel in his own life by experiencing encounters with Jesus. He shares in this book what He learned when Jesus became more real to him. Lea delves deeply into the fundamentals of faith, explaining the implications of Christ's sufficiency as the revelation that sets us free and keeps us anchored through life's storms.

Ultimately, Alain reminds us that Jesus is the whole of the equation as he boldly proclaims that humanity was once lost and now found in Christ Jesus.

Heart To Heart

When the chaos of our daily lives become overwhelming, where can we turn for peace and rest? Apostle Alain Lea points to the source of all hope and strength in Heart To Heart, which contains your daily effective prayers that gets limitless results. Some pray to stay sober, centered or solvent. Others when the lump is deemed malignant, when the money runs out before the month does or when the marriage is falling apart.

We all pray for one thing or the other but sometimes words are hard to find when in the middle of chaos. We are not the first to struggle with prayer. The first followers of Jesus needed prayer guidance too. In fact, prayer is the only tutorial they ever requested and Jesus gave them a prayer, not a lecture on prayer, not the doctrine of prayer; He gave them a quotable, repeatable, portable prayer. Couldn't we use the same today?

In this book, Apostle Alain Lea invites readers on a journey into the very heart of God regarding having a real conversation with Him, offering confidence and hope for doubts, even for prayer wimps. Distilling prayers in the bible down to one pocket-sized prayer book, Alain Lea reminds readers that prayer is not a privilege for the pious nor the art of a chosen few. Prayer is simply a heartfelt conversation between God and His child. Let the conversation begin!

Books Coming Soon

Knowing God in Christ

Our personalities inevitably conform to our god. We have witnessed this down through history. When we worship inferior versions of God. i.e. money, status, security, power, pleasure, you name it – we become like our idols. If your god is money, you will become materialistic. If your god is sex, you will become increasingly sensual. If your god is yourself, you will become more self-focused.

So, this book answers questions like: What is the real nature of God? Is He harsh, as viewed through many Old Testament instances, or is He meek, loving, and gentle of heart, as Jesus portrays? Get ready for a journey into the very heart of the Father, Son and Holy Spirit. This teaching will challenge most of the misconceptions about the being and nature of God. You will be left with a much accurate understanding of who God is, who you are and how you fit in the romance of the ages.

The Void II

The saga continues as life pulls these friends apart, in the midst of dealing with tragedy and the trauma arising from their individual choices and the battle to fill the Void within.